CASTLEBRIDGE HALL
CONSEQUENCES

Michaela Francis

CASTLEBRIDGE HALL CONSEQUENCES

SILVER MOON
ADULT FICTION

A SILVER MOON BOOKS PAPERBACK

ISBN: 978 1 78695 370 4

Silver Moon Books is an imprint of
Fiction4All

Published 2020
Fiction4All

CHAPTER 1

The week, at the end of June, that saw the beating of Brenda Brideshead in the great library of Castlebridge Hall, was notable for the unseasonal warmth of the weather. The English climate seemed to have taken leave of its customary common sense and inflicted week after week of searing temperatures upon a population more habituated to its usual, nondescript and bland uniformity. Barely a whisper of breeze stirred the leaves of the poplars lining the drive, beyond the gates of Castlebridge Hall, and the early summer flowers wilted in their beds beneath the relentless assault of solar radiation. Even the massive stone edifice of Castlebridge Hall itself, built in solid defiance of all the usual vagaries of the country's climate, seemed to droop visibly under this unexpected onslaught of blistering heat. It shimmered resignedly, amidst the extensive parklands, themselves parched arid by weeks of drought, and waited stoically for the blissful anointment of cooling rain to alleviate its misery.

Had such scorching weather had the decency to grace the shores of the Côte d'Azur or cast its favour upon the beaches of the Costa Brava, then doubtless the inhabitants would have welcomed it. The tourists would have flocked in thankful hordes to worship it; the café owners would have put out tables, chairs and parasols on the front terraces of their establishments in anticipation of brisk business; the ice cream vendors would have laid on extra stocks with high hopes of profitable enterprise to come; the tour operators would have cancelled all leave and expected fat bonuses. In other words, all would have been as it should be and the blazing sunshine a blessing upon the venerable vocation of separating tourists from their disposable income. But this wasn't the South of France or Spain. This was Castlebridge Hall, the ancient country seat of the Earls of Castlebridge, set in magnificent splendour amidst the gentle green hills of southern England, and, whilst a day or two of pleasant weather might be looked upon with favour, this interminable heat wave was about as welcome as a blizzard in Benidorm.

The intolerable temperatures had had the most deplorable effects upon the normally rigid discipline within the solid masonry of the Hall and that, by and by, meant the discipline among its womenfolk. The enormous architectural artefact required a large labour force to maintain it in the manner to which the current Lord Castlebridge was accustomed and it was a peculiarity of the Hall that that labour force was mostly female. Many a visitor to the Hall was struck by the contrast of the Hall's outer appearance and the composition of its inhabitants. From the outside, the Hall, with its solid uncompromising stone work, appeared to be a fortress of masculinity yet, penetrate within, and you would discover that this seeming bastion of manhood was an illusion and that by far the majority of everybody you would encounter therein was female and, it has to be said, mostly young and of personable appearance to boot.

This is not to say however that the Hall was in any way a haven of feminine equality. Far from it! With the exception of Mrs Moorhouse, the head of the housekeeping department and the figure of Lord Castlebridge's wife, the senior personnel of the hall were exclusively male. The head butler was male as were the head gardener, the chef, the head caretaker, the head groundsman and the gamekeeper as well as a handful of others. At the head of this male hierarchy was Lord Castlebridge himself; the latest in a long line of Earls who had ruled with an autocratic authority that had changed little in any fundamental way since the late middle ages.

There were a few junior males such as the young men and boys who assisted in the grounds or worked under the caretaker in the physical maintenance of the buildings. Other than these however, the Hall relied for its upkeep on a small battalion of young housemaids, chambermaids, scullery and kitchen maids, serving girls, stable lasses, laundry maids and even a small clerical department of office girls, to handle the bureaucratic necessities and paperwork inevitably generated by an edifice the size of Castlebridge Hall. This small army of young womanhood took up an entire wing of the Hall for their dormitories, common rooms and dining areas and were to thank for the immaculate condition of the Hall's interior and the smooth efficiency of its domestic service.

If you could see your face in the teak panelling in the hallways it was because some young lady had, that very day, laboured long with rag and polish to achieve that perfection of sheen. Should a gentleman visitor to the Hall require his best evening clothes for dinner that evening then a young maid would scurry along to fetch his vestments to the laundry where another girl would be tasked with the job of brushing his jacket and pressing his trousers whilst her colleague shined his shoes. Should you remark upon the cleanliness of the flagstones of the back veranda overlooking the grounds then you could be assured that there was, some young lady, who had spent her afternoon, on her knees, scrubbing them, to thank for their pristine condition. A serving girl placed your evening meal before you and, should you require something to relax with by the fireside at the conclusion of your meal, then you could be certain that her colleague would appear at your elbow, as if she had sprung up from the floorboards, bearing port and cigars on a silver tray. The Hall ran with an admirable efficiency.

This commendable efficiency was not achieved lightly or without cost however. A tradition of Draconian discipline was inherent in the history of Castlebridge Hall and the current Lord Castlebridge saw no reason to deviate from that tradition or that the implementation of such discipline should be any less efficacious in the present day than it had proved to be for his ancestors of the past. Thus, if you were to admire the spotless cleanliness of the bathroom adjoining your suite, it would be because the chamber maid, tasked with the duty of cleaning it, would be all too aware of the painful consequences that a less than assiduous application of that duty would entail. Conversely, were you to run a finger along a mantelpiece and remark that the place seemed rather dusty, then the consequences of your observation would filter down the chain of command, leading to recriminations in the house keeping department, stern admonitions and all too likely to result in the maid responsible for the negligence being called upon to answer for her dereliction by bending over with her skirts and petticoats raised, her knickers lowered to her knees and receiving whatever punishment was deemed appropriate by her superiors to her bare backside.

For minor infractions this punishment would normally be a matter of internal departmental discipline. Mrs Moorhouse, the head housekeeper, for instance, would generally deal with such small infractions herself and chastise the young ladies in her charge on the spot without recourse to higher authority. She favoured the use of thick leather straps for this purpose although, when she felt it merited, would occasionally utilise a martinet which, being a short, multi-tailed whip was an instrument much to be feared.

Whilst these measures were considered sufficient for lesser offences and for general maintenance discipline, more serious matters were referred to the Hall's head butler, Mr Greenwood. Greenwood was an imposing gentleman of large stature, majestic bearing and formidable authority. His favoured instrument of choice in disciplinary matters was the rattan cane of which he had a considerable selection; all carefully chosen and fashioned with stout grips by himself. His height and build lent considerable force to cane wielded in his hands and few of the woeful culprits among the domestic staff that had suffered the misfortune to experience the agonising effect of his cane felt in any hurry to be re-acquainted with it.

Routine canings of anything up to around twenty five or thirty strokes of the cane were generally administered in the nearest convenient space with the miscreant in question being merely required to raise her skirts, lower her knickers and assume the customary position for punishment. In most cases, thirty strokes was considered the absolute maximum that any young offender could be expected to endure whilst still retaining her position obediently for the duration of the caning and there were many, it has to be said, that could not even withstand that many, such was the excruciating pain of the cane across the bare flesh when administered by Greenwood's strong right hand. For punishments beyond routine correction therefore, other measures were regarded as necessary requirements.

For those offences deemed particularly serious, matters of repeated offences or those indicative of a long pattern of misconduct the consequences were commensurately severe. Such matters might see the culprit called upon to answer for the failures in her conduct with a severe flogging that could, and frequently did, amount to fifty or more strokes of the cane. Such a caning was a fearful ordeal and not even the most hardened or compliantly obedient servant girl could be expected to submissively maintain the correct position for the receipt of her caning under the frightful agony of such a beating.

Such severe punishments, therefore, were considered formal affairs and conducted in the Hall's library which, over the generations, had, by tradition, come to be accepted as the chamber within the Hall where disciplinary hearings of a more formal and serious nature were conducted and the subsequent punishments administered. Aside from the now rarely used ballroom, the library was the largest room in the Hall. It was a high chamber with great vaulting eaves spanned by massive oaken beams, furnished with solid wooden chairs and tables and lined with acres of bookshelves containing thousands of weighty tomes. Being at a remove from the more frequented regions of the Hall and with its stern and austere manner, the library was an admirable place in which to address matters of the most serious misconduct or dereliction of duty. Amongst the servant girls of Castlebridge Hall, a summons to report to the library for punishment was the most dreaded fate of all. For the young lady thus summonsed, making her way through the galleries of the Hall, her face pale with fear, trembling with dread anticipation and with tears pricking at her eyes, such a summons almost invariably meant, a soon to be, intimate acquaintance with the library's caning stool; the venerable, solid oak apparatus which had graced the library far beyond the living memory of anybody in the Hall and over which generations of wretched domestic servants had been strapped down, in immobility, to learn the errors of their ways and rue the consequences of their misbehaviour.

All these disciplinary functions had been much in evidence over the past weeks and for that the unusual weather was largely to blame. Work at Castlebridge Hall was hard and demanding at the best of times. Under the insufferable heatwave gripping the southern counties of England it was tantamount to purgatory. Inevitably a stupefying languor had descended over the Hall and the normal rigorous application to duty of the domestic staff had suffered as a result. Under the arduous conditions, corners had been cut. Some duties had received only perfunctory attention and others had been neglected altogether. The girls of Castlebridge Hall had grown indolent and slothful under the burden of the incessant heat; grumbling and insubordination had become endemic and tempers become more frayed the longer the intolerable heat continued.

A more compassionate or sympathetic master than Lord Castlebridge would have understood that the decline in the usual high standards was attributable to the unusual circumstances and perhaps tolerated a certain temporary laxness among his domestic staff as a result of the weather. His Lordship's own temper, however, had not been improved by day after day of scorching heat and, with several worrying matters concerning him in his business dealings, the evidence of the less than satisfactory performance of his household maids had only served to irritate him further. As a result he had summonsed his senior staff and demanded that the decline be arrested forthwith and that stern measures be taken immediately to correct the perceptible idleness and negligence currently prevailing among the staff.

Evidence of this rigorous cracking of the collective whip was presently to be found in one of the downstairs drawing rooms where a certain young Peggy Monsworth was currently to be found bent over the arm of a stout leather arm chair having her bottom strapped by Mrs Moorhouse. Peggy was, in common with most of the girls at Castlebridge Hall, an attractive young lady. If there was a fault to be perceived in her appearance then it could most properly be attributed to Peggy's weakness for sweet confectionery. This weakness led her too easily to the side of plumpness. It was not that she was obese by any measure. A hard working life at Castlebridge Hall precluded that. She was merely apt to become a little chubby about the waist or hindquarters. It was this unfortunate proclivity that lay at the root of her present predicament.

The previous week Lord Castlebridge had conducted one of his periodic inspections of the Hall, accompanied by Mrs Moorhouse. They had come across Peggy in the Long Gallery, manhandling a heavy mahogany desk aside in order to dust behind it. Peggy had been perspiring heavily, which had been hardly surprising considering the weight of the desk and the ambient temperature at the time. Lord Castlebridge, on the other hand, had placed a rather more personal interpretation upon Peggy's struggles; preferring in fact to believe that they were more due to a lamentable lack of physical fitness on her part. She, he opined, appeared to be putting a lot of weight on.

Lord Castlebridge was particularly strict in this respect. Not only were the girls of Castlebridge Hall under exacting rules concerning their work and personal conduct but even their health and physical condition was monitored closely. Lord Castlebridge had narrowed his eyes at Peggy's seemingly excess pounds and felt it indicative of the atmosphere of indolence currently infecting the Hall. In order to confirm his suspicions, he had ordered Peggy to remove her clothes in order to examine her. Blushing scarlet with humiliation, poor Peggy had complied, stripping her maid's uniform and underwear off under Lord Castlebridge's critical eye. Once she was naked Lord Castlebridge had walked around her slowly, grunting with disapproval. He had even gone so far as to poke her. Finally he had turned to Mrs Moorhouse and declared that the girl was clearly overweight and had adjured Mrs Moorhouse to see to the matter.

The result of this mortifying indignity was that Peggy had been placed on a strict diet. Peggy was a girl with a healthy appetite and the diet had been torment thus far. She had been perpetually hungry all week and Mrs Moorhouse had rather suspected her of cheating on her diet. Those suspicions had been confirmed when Mrs Moorhouse, on her rounds, had caught Peggy red handed with a pair of chocolate bars in her apron pocket. After that discovery there had been nothing for it but to order Peggy to raise her skirts, lower her knickers and prostrate herself over the armchair. Peggy had a pretty face but that prettiness was not in evidence at the moment, being contorted in a grimace of pain, streaked with tears and with a crimson hue to match that of her possibly overly plump buttocks wobbling under the stinging blows of Mrs Moorhouse's strap.

It had seen much sterling service of late, that strap. In addition to Peggy, no less than five other girls had been on the receiving end of it in the last ten days alone. Nor was that all. Only the night before, Mrs Moorhouse had conducted a late night round of the servants' wing and caught two young maids sneaking down a corridor in their nightgowns, well after lights out and at an hour when regulations demanded that they be tucked up in their beds in their dormitories. Their excuse that they were merely visiting the lavatory was transparently false for there was a lavatory adjoining their dormitory and they were not even on the same floor! Entirely dissatisfied with their explanations, Mrs Moorhouse had marched the pair of them off to her own chambers where she had ordered them to remove their nightgowns and spent five minutes whipping their backs and buttocks with the martinet before ordering them back to bed.

Mrs Moorhouse had never got to the bottom of why the two girls had been abroad at that hour but she suspected that they had been on their way to a clandestine encounter. What such an encounter might have been was open to speculation. The worst case was that possibly the encounter may have involved men.

In the strictly regimented life of the Castlebridge Hall servants, contact with the opposite sex was severely limited. In effect it was restricted to those hours of freedom afforded by their afternoons off or their free days. Even these interludes afforded little opportunity for romantic liaisons. On their afternoons off, the girls might well walk down to the village for a few hours of leisure but they were under strict curfew to be back before ten o'clock and, in any case, Mrs Moorhouse had enough spies in the village to report any unseemly dilly-dallying with the village lads. Their days off might have provided greater opportunities but even these were limited. The girls would frequently take the bus to town on their days off and hope for some romantic adventure far from the omnipresent view of the Halls' authorities. Sadly the last bus back to Castlebridge in the evening was at eight o'clock and it was a caning offence to miss it. It hardly lent itself to nights of wild adventure.

Strictly prohibited was any fraternisation with any of the young men working around the Hall other than that deemed unavoidable in the course of one's duties. This decree had its genesis in a scandal that had rocked the household many years before when one of the chamber maids had become pregnant following an affair with one of the gardener's assistants. Now there was a tightly controlled separation between the sexes. The boys on the estates had their own quarters in a converted barn down near the old mill in the grounds and were not even allowed to set foot in the main Hall except on those occasions when it was absolutely necessary. The girls for their part were mostly restricted to the garden areas immediately closest to the Hall although they were allowed, on occasions, to take walks in the park lands or even picnic down by the lake albeit only under close chaperone.

Of course these regulations were frequently transgressed. The girls had been sneaking down the old fire escape in the servants' wing for clandestine midnight trysts with their paramours since time out of mind at Castlebridge Hall. It was a dangerous occupation however for the penalties for being caught were severe. Only the month before, one of the maids had been caught in a state of partial undress in a hayloft with one of the delivery boys from the bakery. The boy had been banned in perpetuity from setting foot on the estate forthwith and the young maid in question had been ordered to the library for a salutary caning.

It might be thought, therefore, that these regulations, by so severely curtailing the occasions for romantic outlet, would result in a body of very frustrated young ladies in the Hall. Such, however, was not the case. The girls simply transferred their frustrated affections to each other. They were, after all, healthy young ladies with correspondingly healthy appetites and, if the pleasures of young men were denied to them, there were always their sisters in servitude to provide pleasant compensation. Indeed it might be said that their dalliances with each other were the favourite leisure activities among the girls of Castlebridge Hall and it would be a brave person indeed that attempted to unravel the labyrinthine complexities of romantic life among them.

Oddly enough, this was one area where the girls were less strictly controlled. It was not that it was officially tolerated as such. Any girls caught playing with each other would certainly have been in contravention of the rules and would face punishment. It was more a case that the senior staff tended to turn a blind eye to this particular aspect of the girls' conduct. The reasons for this were complicated. For one thing it was considered an inevitability of the girls' close life together with each other. They worked together; they ate together; they shared dormitories together; it was unavoidable that they would therefore play together.

Nor was this entirely considered to be altogether a bad thing. Even Lord Castlebridge himself recognised that the girls had to have some sort of outlet for their romantic passions and that efforts to curtail the sexual drives of a horde of young women were about as likely to succeed as King Canute's endeavours in the field of tidal engineering. Their love affairs with each other at least provided a safety valve for their urges and, furthermore, had the virtue of being relatively harmless in that they carried no threat of unwanted pregnancy and little chance of sexually transmitted disease.

Another reason for overlooking this particular aspect of the girls' lives was entirely pragmatic. It was a question of staff morale. The girls could be fiercely devoted and passionate towards their girlfriends and any attempt to sever the relationships between them would lead to a crash in morale among them and most probably precipitate outright rebellion. It was a wise eye, therefore, that blinkered itself to their complex and multifaceted love lives and let well alone. Only in cases where there had been a flagrant act, impossible to overlook, or those instances where the interminable infidelities, petty jealousies or squabbling over girlfriends threatened to disrupt domestic harmony, was the issue addressed at all and action taken. Otherwise the girls were left largely to their own devices in this regard and the servants' wing was such a resultant hotbed of ever changing liaisons, love triangles, clandestine meetings, devoted declarations, theatrical drama and trappings of passion that even the poetess Sappho would have thrown up her hands in despair.

There was one final reason why such activity was generally regarded as being one in which it was considered unwise to delve into too closely. It was the fact that the first lady of the household, Lady Castlebridge in person, was by no means immune to such a proclivity herself. It would have been hypocritical at best and downright risky at worst to proscribe an indulgence that Her Ladyship too was wont to seek gratification in. Few would dare to question Her Ladyship's private affairs. Even her husband, with his own skeletons in the cupboard, tended to treat his wife's diversions with her personal handmaidens with studied, benign neglect.

This is not to say that Lady Castlebridge could do as she wanted by any means. On the contrary, there were many areas of misconduct for which she could be mostly definitely taken to account. It was one of these instances of misconduct that would emerge this day and, as Castlebridge Hall sweltered under the heat of June, the consequences of that misconduct would provide a fitting prelude to the memorable week which would see Brenda Brideshead's caning at Castlebridge Hall.

CHAPTER 2

At the same time as poor Peggy Monsworth was squealing under the ministrations of Mrs Moorhouse's strap, Lady Castlebridge, in her private boudoir, was listening to an entirely more agreeable squealing. The source of this pleasant, if not particularly musical, emanation of sound was Lady Castlebridge's personal maid, Suzette, and the reason for her excited squeals and whimpers was not difficult to discern. Suzette was lying naked on a thick rug with her legs apart. Face down between those spread limbs, with her dark tresses draped over Suzette's thighs and her face buried deep in Suzette's intimate regions, was the equally naked Maria, the other of Her Ladyship's favourite hand maidens. Maria's wickedly darting tongue was teasing wails and shrieks of ever-increasing volume from Suzette and driving all sense and reason from her mind as she surrendered to its delightful caresses.

Lady Castlebridge reclined on a low chaise lounge and watched her two maids with fond affection. She was clad, although just barely, in a short, silk negligee of lustrous pearl and matching knickers. Clutched in her left hand was a disgracefully early glass of sherry whilst her right hand lay hidden beneath the waistband of her knickers, stroking her sex with its fingertips, to enhance Her Ladyship's enjoyment of the spectacle being enacted before her.

Lady Castlebridge loved to watch her two young ladies enjoy each other in this fashion and the sight of the two beautiful naked girls together in such uninhibited embrace invariably aroused her. She would often command them to perform for her therefore and the two girls, who adored their beautiful and benevolent mistress, would eagerly comply to her wishes as she watched them in pleasure, occasionally interrupting to furnish instructions or perhaps to command them to move slightly, the better to display whatever it was they happened to be doing for Her Ladyship's gratification. She would lie at her ease, stroking herself and observing them closely, with immense satisfaction, until she had drunk her fill of the sight of them or until such time that her own needs had reached such a state of urgency that she was compelled to command them to abandon their caresses of each other and attend to her in person.

It was well that Lady Castlebridge's private chambers were set high in a separate wing of the Hall and so far removed from the rest of the household, for little Suzette was not the quietest of girls in the throes of passion. Suzette hailed from the Provence in Southern France and apt to punctuate her frenzied wails and squeals with a fevered gibberish in her native tongue during the consummation of such intimate acts. "Ah non!" she pleaded in desperation as Maria's ministrations threatened to rob her of what little reason remained to her. "Arrête toi! Ah Mon Dieu! Avoir pitié s'il tu plaît! Je vais defaillir!"

Her own excitement increasing, Lady Castlebridge grinned and closed her ears to Suzette's imprecations for mercy. "A little faster if you please Maria." she commanded. "I want to see her come. I'll give you fifty pounds bonus on your allowance this week if she faints dead away!" Spurred on by this incentive, Maria doubled her efforts and Suzette's shrieks reached a manic pitch. "Nearly there I think." urged Lady Castlebridge. "One last little push Maria." Maria obediently nuzzled closer, gripping Suzette's hips and holding her tight to her questing tongue until she felt the French girl's muscles tauten in a spasm. Suzette grasped Maria's hair in her climax, arched her back up off the rug, threw her head back and, with her face flushed crimson in ultimate arousal, opened her mouth wide to let vent to a long ululating wail as the scorching orgasm racked her body in exquisite torment and soaked Maria's face in a gush of liquid.

As Suzette collapsed senseless on the rug, in what her native language would describe as "Le petit mort", Lady Castlebridge's hand quickened beneath the silk of her boudoir knickers. She gasped as she drenched the crotch of her knickers and spilled half her sherry down the front of her negligee while matching Suzette's orgasm with her own.

Catching her breath, Lady Castlebridge laid her glass aside with trembling fingers. She clapped her hands gently in appreciative applause. "Well done Maria." she praised warmly. "That was wonderful!" She gazed fondly at the prostrate figure of Suzette, whimpering feebly on the floor and pawing helplessly at the rug. "She's ruined beyond redemption! You're getting very good at that."

"Thank you My Lady." Maria simpered under

her mistress's praise.

"Fetch the adorable little slut over here so I can give both of you a big kiss for being good girls."

Maria grinned and dragged the feebly protesting Suzette across the rug to Lady Castlebridge's feet where the pair of them squatted at her knees. Lady Castlebridge kissed them in great affection and stroked the tangled ruins of their hair fondly. She ran a finger down the side of Suzette's face. "Dear me, ma cherie." she murmured, "You are *so* noisy! Half the Hall must have heard you. I really will have to consider gagging you before letting Maria work on you in future."

Maria rubbed her scalp ruefully. "Perhaps you'd consider tying her up as well ma'am." she suggested. "She's nearly torn my hair out by the roots!"

Suzette pouted at Maria. "Et qui est à blâmer pour cette, Nom de Dieu? Putain!"

Lady Castlebridge affected a look of outrage and clucked her tongue in mock disapproval. "Tut tut Suzette! Your language is becoming most unladylike of late! Am I going to have to discipline you?"

Suzette's doe like, adoring eyes gazed at her mistress imploringly. "Ah oui Madame! I 'ave been very bad girl. S'il vous plaît me punir."

Lady Castlebridge chuckled deeply and patted her knee. "Come along then ma petite nénette." With a sigh of pure joy, Suzette staggered up off her knees and draped herself obediently across Her Ladyship's knee. Lady Castlebridge savoured the sight of Suzette's pert buttocks, quivering in delightful anticipation on her knee, and stroked the smooth rounded orbs lovingly. She glanced at her glass on the little low table at her side and frowned. "I seem to have spilled half my sherry Maria. Be a good girl, will you, and fetch the decanter."

Maria looked uncertain. "You want another sherry My Lady?"

Lady Castlebridge wagged a finger at Maria. "Don't be querying my orders in that disapproving tone Maria or you'll be next over my knee. You're overdue for a good spanking too!"

"I'm sorry ma'am."

Lady Castlebridge smiled. "I know that it's early and that you're concerned sweetheart but I have a trying day to face and I could with a little fortification."

"Trying My Lady?"

"Yes Maria. At some point this afternoon, when my husband returns from the office, I'm going to have to face him and confess that we blew upwards of twelve thousand pounds on the horses at Ascot last week. I should imagine that he will not be best pleased!"

Maria grimaced. "Do you have to tell him My Lady? He might not find out after all."

Lady Castlebridge shook her head regretfully. "Fat chance Maria! There's no way I can hide a hole in my household budget that big. Four or five thousand I might have been able to cover up under sundry expenses but he'll spot a gaping cavity of that size in an instance. In any case Alison Montfort saw us lose all that money and she's bound to tell that foul whore, Emilie Dixon, my husband keeps in his city office when she sees her at the weekend. La Dixon will waste no time whatsoever informing him and I daren't risk him finding out through third parties and adding the sin of deceitfulness to my tally of misconduct. He's going to blow a fuse as it is! That's why I need a drink. In fact to hell with the sherry! I need something a little stronger. Be a good girl and be pouring me out a stiff brandy..." Lady Castlebridge paused to land a hard smack across Suzette's bottom, "while I give this pretty little bottom the spanking it deserves!"

Maria grinned happily. "Yes ma'am." and scuttled away in compliance. A minute or two later she was back with a balloon glass, a third full, of fine cognac and stood waiting patiently with it in her hand as she admired her mistress's handiwork. Suzette was squirming and yelping loudly as Her Ladyship reddened her rump with hard slaps.

Lady Castlebridge looked up from her labour and nodded at the little table. "Just put it down on there Maria if you please."

"Yes ma'am"

Lady Castlebridge paused to run the back of her hand across her forehead. "It's too warm for this sort of work." she observed. "I suppose, in the light of the disaster at Ascot, that this would not be a propitious moment to canvass my husband with a view to him shelling out to have air conditioning installed."

"Perhaps he'll be in a mellow mood and prepared to be lenient My Lady." Maria suggested.

"Well perhaps but I'm not overly optimistic about it. He's been in a foul mood this past couple of weeks and forever bleating about the wretched state of the economy and the need for us to conserve funds." She shook her head sadly and administered another dozen hard smacks to the squealing Suzette's rosy cheeks. She paused again to take a sip of her brandy. "No Maria," she continued, "I'm afraid I'm just going to have to bite the bullet." She sighed heavily and rested a hand on Suzette's bottom, feeling the warmth emanating from the quivering buttocks. "It's not going to be a happy day Maria!"

Suzette was emitting soft moans and panting gently. Lady Castlebridge could perceive an increasing dampness in her lap. She raised an ironic eyebrow and slipped her hand between Suzette's buttocks, seeking out the warm darkness within. She withdrew her hand, slick with moisture from its investigations, and regarded it with wry amusement. "You know Maria, I rather think that this young lady is enjoying this altogether too much. Would you be so kind as to fetch me the hairbrush from my dressing table... the big one with the ivory handle."

CHAPTER 3

Whilst Lord Castlebridge might bemoan the general lassitude and idleness of the Hall's maids as a result of the scorching weather, it has to be said that these were not failings entirely confined to the junior members of the household. Even Mr Greenwood, the rock upon which Lord Castlebridge founded the disciplinary foundations of the Hall, was not immune from a certain lethargy precipitated by the intolerable temperatures or entirely innocent of avoiding the most taxing of duties during the heat of the afternoon. Indeed, even as Lady Castlebridge paddled her maid in her boudoir, Greenwood was taking his ease in the wine cellar adjoining his pantry. This was the one part of the Hall that could be counted on to be cool and a sanctuary from the sultry torridity pervading the rest of the house.

Greenwood was ostensibly "stock taking" but it was a transparent pretext. In point of fact he was reclining in a battered old leather armchair, with his jacket draped over the back, and refreshing himself with a draught of cool ale that he had drawn straight from one of the barrels in the cellar. Greenwood had found the weather of late particularly trying. Although, during his younger days with the Royal Artillery, he had been obliged to serve in countries with a warm climate he was not a man that took kindly to hot weather. It was especially arduous attending to his duties whilst clad in the customary garb of head butler, with its heavy dark jacket and waistcoat, stiff collared shirt and bow tie, and Greenwood looked forward, with ever increasingly eager anticipation, to his annual summer leave which would commence the following week.

Greenwood allowed himself to dwell pleasurably on the thought of his coming leave. It was his custom to take his summer vacation in the Western Highlands of Scotland where he would spend the days in healthy outdoor activities such as fell walking in the mountains or fishing for trout in the lochs and burns. He could barely wait for his holidays to begin. Surely, he reassured himself, the weather would be far more agreeable. Southern England might disgrace itself with this unseemly display of swarthy Mediterranean madness but surely good old Scotland could be relied upon to maintain some sort of decorum and remain true to its reputation for dour bracing climate. Last year, on his annual holiday, it had rained for at least half the time. Greenwood hadn't been that put out by it since it had afforded him the opportunity to indulge in another of his hobbies involving the interior of cosy public houses and the imbibing of fine malt whiskeys, of which he was somewhat of a connoisseur. He had grumbled a little about the rain at the time to be sure but, after these past weeks, he would count his blessings if it rained every day. Come to that he wouldn't mind in the least if it *snowed*!

There was only one worry about his forthcoming annual leave and that revolved around the matter of his replacement. For the duration of the three weeks annually that he spent idling his time away in Scotland, Greenwood was obliged to find a locum to cover his duties for the period of his absence. The previous year, his temporary replacement had been entirely unsatisfactory. He had been a young man from an employment agency who had spent most of his employment in the Hall steadily working his way through the contents of Greenwood's liquor stores. He had performed his routine duties in the most perfunctory of manners and neglected anything beyond the most basic necessities of his function.

Worst of all, in many respects, he had failed entirely to execute the disciplinary duties, incumbent upon the position, with the result that the junior household staff had taken Greenwood's absence to be the equivalent of a holiday of their own. Discipline had collapsed for the duration and Greenwood had returned from his leave to find a disgraceful tally of neglect, misconduct and subordination. Lord Castlebridge had been furious and Greenwood had spent much of the week, following his return, thrashing the worst offenders in the library.

He had determined that there would be no such repetition this year. To avoid it, he had acquired the services of the junior butler at Torsbury Towers who served as an understudy to an old friend of his. His friend had spoken highly of the young gentleman's sober seriousness and diligent application to duty while generously sparing him to cover Greenwood's annual leave. Greenwood had been deeply grateful and had promised his friend a crate of Aberfeldy malt from Scotland upon his return.

The only fly in the ointment of this agreeable arrangement was that Greenwood's friend was unable to release his understudy until the very day that Greenwood was due to depart for Scotland. Since Greenwood would be taking the early morning train that day, it would afford him no time to properly acquaint the young man with his duties. Fortunately, the young gentleman, who appeared to be possessed of a most conscientious sense of obligation, had volunteered to come to the Hall, this very afternoon, on his day off, in order to be fully apprised, in advance, of the responsibilities that would fall to him over the period that he would be acting as locum at the Hall. Greenwood was expecting the young man any minute and had left word as to where he could be found upon the gentleman's arrival.

When the young maid knocked on the door of Greenwood's pantry to announce that there was a Mr Fletcher waiting in the staff entrance hall to see him, Greenwood glanced at his watch in agreeable surprise. The young man was certainly punctual; indeed he was five minutes early. "Thank you young lady." he told the maid. "Please offer Mr Fletcher some refreshment and inform him that I shall be with him presently."

Five minutes later, Greenwood strode into the staff reception area to discover a serious looking young man perched on the edge of a chair clutching a tumbler of iced lemon tea. The young man sprung to his feet as Greenwood approached and thrust out a hand. "Good afternoon sir." he intoned politely. "You must be Mr Greenwood."

Greenwood took the proffered hand and inclined his head gravely. "Yes and you, I take it, must be Mr

Fletcher."

The young man nodded eagerly. "At your service sir. I'm very pleased to meet you."

Greenwood regarded the young man in appreciation. He liked what he saw. Certainly the young man took his obligations seriously. It was theoretically the young man's day off and, given the scorching temperature, he could have been forgiven for dressing in a more casual and comfortable fashion. In spite of that however, young Mr Fletcher had not stinted in his adherence to correct dress code, turning up in the full costume appropriate to his position as a junior butler. Greenwood was impressed. "Thank you for coming up on your free day Mr Fletcher. I apologise for the inconvenience."

The young man dismissed Greenwood's apologies without hesitation. "Not at all sir. It was the least I could do. My only concern is that there is little time for you to familiarise me with those duties expected of me when I'm required here next week. I hope that I can learn them quickly. I would not wish to give anything less than complete satisfaction sir."

Greenwood nodded in approval, liking this young man more by the second. "Your dedication is admirable Mr Fletcher and Mr Arkwright speaks most highly of you. I am sure we will have no grounds for dissatisfaction in your instance."

"Thank you for your confidence in me sir."

"Not at all. Now to business if we may." Greenwood held out a slim notebook. "Now I have written down in detail your duties and responsibilities in this small book Mr Fletcher. You might wish to take it with you and study it at your leisure."

The young man took the notebook with a slight bow. "Thank you sir. That will be most helpful."

"I do hope so. It is, I believe, fairly comprehensive. However I think it will be of great assistance to you if I were to conduct you on a tour of the Hall, with particular emphasis on those parts which will fall under your jurisdiction, in order to better familiarise you with your duties and those areas and stocks which are most pertinent to them."

"I would like that sir."

"Excellent. In that case... if you would follow me."

For the next two hours, Greenwood led his young replacement around the Hall, instructing him in the areas of his responsibility. The young man listened attentively and even jotted down some notes in the book Greenwood had provided him with. Greenwood grew more and more confident that securing the young Mr Fletcher's services had been an inspired move. They spent some considerable time in the pantry and wine cellars, as Greenwood familiarised his protégée with the considerable stocks. "I have written down the exact location of the most important items in that modest guide I provided you with Mr Fletcher." Greenwood informed him. "I trust it will cover most contingencies."

"Yes sir. I understand that your private chambers abut the pantry as well sir."

"Yes but, for the duration of your stay with us, I have instructed the housekeeping department to prepare a guest room in the senior servant's wing. It is a pleasant enough room and I trust you will be comfortable there."

"I'm sure it will be satisfactory sir." The young man nodded at the door. "I suppose the doors to these chambers are kept locked sir."

Greenwood pursed his lips. The young man had touched on a sore point. "Yes, naturally, and you will be provided with the keys." Greenwood paused for a moment. "However I must inform you that, in spite of these precautions, there is still a considerable amount of petty pilfering of alcoholic beverages from the stores. You would be well advised to be vigilant in this regard Mr Fletcher."

The young man looked shocked. "Really sir? I confess I am astonished. If the doors are kept locked who could be responsible for this outrage and how?"

Greenwood looked at the young man sadly. "I fear that there may be a number of duplicate keys in circulation about the Hall Mr Fletcher. How they have come into being is a mystery. Petty theft among the maids remains a considerable headache I'm afraid to say."

"That's deplorable sir!"

"It is certainly reprehensible I grant you. I had the locks changed only six months ago and I thought that would put a stop to it. I was to be sadly disillusioned however. Within a few short weeks the problem was as bad as ever and I was forced to conclude that the security of the new locks had been as thoroughly compromised as the old."

"You mean that there were already new duplicate

keys in existence?"

"I'm afraid that would be my analysis, yes. Just how it occurred I am at a loss to explain. I regret to say that, among the young ladies in service here at the Hall, there are far too many whose ingenuity is not matched by commensurate integrity."

"You astound me sir. I would hope that the severest measures are taken should those responsible be discovered."

"Indeed yes and that brings us nicely to the final one of your duties that I wish to discuss with you. It is an important duty if a somewhat disagreeable one. I refer to the disciplinary function expected of the Hall's butler."

"Disciplinary function sir?"

"Yes Mr Fletcher. Although much routine discipline is dealt with by other senior members of the staff, the task of administering more formal disciplinary actions devolves on the person of the head butler."

"So Mr Arkwright led me to understand sir. However, as a mere locum and understudy, I didn't expect that that duty would fall within my sphere of responsibility sir."

Greenwood nodded in concern. "I see. I take it then that you are not called upon to discipline junior members of the household at Torsbury Towers."

The young man shook his head. "No sir. Mr Arkwright, as head butler, usually deals with those matters. I'm afraid that I wouldn't feel at all confident in executing those responsibilities."

"I see." Greenwood repeated. "I'm afraid that this task would fall within your province here at

Castlebridge Hall however. Since you would be standing in as head butler here, then this is a function that would most properly be your area of responsibility. On previous occasions when I have been away, the absence of a strong disciplinary hand has led to a lamentable increase in disorder and misbehaviour. I was rather hoping that you would feel comfortable in exercising a firm disciplinary role therefore. Of course I would not expect you to deal with serious matters of gross misconduct but I had rather hoped that you would at least be able to handle more general infractions and mete out appropriate punishments for them, as and when required."

Mr Fletcher bit his lip worriedly. "Well sir I would try to do my best but I'm afraid that I have little experience in these matters."

"I quite understand." Greenwood thought for a moment or two. "Well perhaps I may be able to give you some guidance in this direction. If you'll follow me I'll take you to the library."

The two men ventured once more into the labyrinthine corridors and galleries of the Hall. At the massive wooden doors of the library, Greenwood paused to address his junior colleague. "I must apologise in advance for the dishevelled state of the library at the moment Mr Fletcher. We have workmen in, affecting some much needed repairs and restoration, this week and I'm afraid the place is in a bit of a mess."

"Quite all right sir. Old houses such as this need considerable amounts of maintenance, as I know only too well from Torsbury Towers."

"Quite so. Well if you would care to step inside." The library was indeed in a deranged state, the massive antique furniture stacked at one end and covered in dust sheets and with tools and materials littering the ancient parquet floor which itself looked untidy beneath a light covering of sawdust and wood chippings. Greenwood frowned. "It appears that the workmen have finished for the day or might possibly be taking a break." he observed. "Well at least we shan't be disturbed." Picking his way through the detritus, he led his colleague to a tall slender cabinet set into the wall. He opened this cabinet to reveal a row of lengths of rattan cane hanging on hooks within by way of leather loops attached to the leather grips that formed their handles. "These are the instruments I normally employ in corrective discipline." he began by way of explanation. "Other senior staff members have their own methods but I favour the use of the cane. I find it the most efficacious method of inflicting the desirable degree of chastisement, required in most instances, to impress upon the miscreant the standards of conduct and deportment this house expects of them. A lesson reinforced with a good stout length of cane is one rarely forgotten Mr Fletcher." Greenwood paused to regard the younger man in some concern. "I assume, from what you have already told me, that you have not, in the course of your duties, been hitherto obliged to administer a caning."

The young man shook his head regretfully. "I'm afraid nor sir. I have, on occasion, been privileged to observe Mr Arkwright's technique when he was called upon to correct one of the maids at Torsbury Towers sir but I'm afraid my experience goes no further than that."

Greenwood nodded gravely. "I see. Well I think it high time that you were taught the basics at least Mr Fletcher. Mr Arkwright is, after all, advanced in years and nearing retirement. I understand that you are being groomed as his successor at Torsbury Towers and it is therefore imperative that you be fully abreast of all the duties of head butler before such time as you are obliged to take over the reins of command as it were. Your period as locum here will be valuable training for the day when you inherit such high responsibility."

"Mr Arkwright said much the same thing sir."

"I'm gratified to hear it." Greenwood turned his attention back to the row of canes. "Now the correcting of some young lady's misconduct with the cane may not be the most pleasant of duties we are compelled to perform Mr Fletcher but it is an essential one. One cannot expect to be able to retain decorum and acceptable behaviour in a household as large as this, or Torsbury Towers for that matter, without firm standards of discipline and the promise of stern retribution for anybody transgressing those standards. Indeed it is as well, should one desire to maintain harmony and tranquillity in the house, to make frequent use of the cane. In point of fact, His Lordship, here at the Hall, is a firm believer that the young ladies, in service here, should be beaten regularly whether they have merited it or not. I do not necessarily subscribe to that opinion myself, for the most part, although we do set aside two or three days a year for a general flogging of all the junior servants and I am compelled to admit that the house is remarkably quiet and well behaved for some time afterwards."

Greenwood paused in his explanations to pluck a pair of canes down from their hooks. He handed one of these implements to his junior colleague who regarded it somewhat nervously. "Perhaps you would care to examine the canes we use here Mr Fletcher." he offered. "I make these canes to my own specifications. You will note that they are generally about a quarter of an inch thick. If they are much thicker than that the striking area is too broad and you don't get the concentration of impact in a narrow streak that is so painful and is the cane's greatest virtue. On the other hand I don't favour canes that are too thin. Thin canes don't have the weight and authority to maximise the painful effects of a well delivered stroke."

"I see sir. These canes seem rather longer than the ones Mr Arkwright employs."

"I'm pleased that you noticed that Mr Fletcher. I am a great advocate of longer canes. I feel that many people use canes that are far too short in my opinion. I rarely use canes shorter than about five feet in length and my longest, reserved for severe punishments, are closer to six feet in length. A long cane has much more weight behind it and the longer length means it proscribes a greater arc in the swing, resulting in a harder impact on the target. Up to a point, the longer a cane is, the more painful its effect although very long canes become somewhat unwieldy beyond a certain length."

Greenwood patted the handle of the cane he was holding. "You'll note too that I have my canes fashioned with a leather grip on the end. A good grip facilitates a firm and accurate delivery, I find. It also makes them easier to hang up because of the leather loop on the grip. Canes should always be hung where possible. Canes that are stood up against a wall or in a receptacle tend to warp in time and it can be the ruin of a good cane. I'm a believer in maintaining the condition of my canes. All my canes are soaked in linseed oil once a year and every month I give them a quick two or three minute soak in lukewarm water to maintain their suppleness and avoid them drying out. It is important to allow them to dry in the open air after a soaking, otherwise they may become mouldy."

"I see sir. Most instructive. I had no idea that there was so much involved."

"Yes indeed Mr Fletcher. A sound cane will afford you years of sterling service if it is well cared for." Greenwood stroked the cane in his hand lovingly before shaking his head. "But that is enough about the actual implements for the time being. I think a little practical experience would be judicious at this juncture. Would you follow me please and bring that cane with you?"

Before leaving the library, Greenwood stopped to point out a slightly lighter patch on the parquet in the centre of the big room. "This is where the caning stool normally stands." he explained. "In cases when severe canings are called for, the miscreant is punished formally here in the library and immobilised with straps over the caning stool.

This, I emphasise, is the punishment reserved for serious offences with sentences usually in excess of forty or fifty strokes being deemed warranted. Since we have the workmen in the library this week I have had the caning stool removed and placed in my pantry. You will not be required to use the apparatus in any case. It is, as I say, reserved for severe punishments and, given your inexperience, I would not expect you to administer such a punishment. If there are any offences that occur, during your period of locum, that you feel exceed your authority to deal with, then I would be grateful if you would write up a report on them and I shall see to the culprits on my return from Scotland. Now if you'll come with me please."

CHAPTER 4

Back out of the library, the two men wandered the corridors of the Hall seemingly at random and, before long, the young Mr Fletcher felt quite lost and beginning to wonder if there was any point to this apparently meaningless meandering. However, as they entered a broad gallery lined with grim looking portraits, they spied a young maid, clad in the standard dress of short black, low cut Maid's dress, with white cap, frilled apron and the frilly hem of her petticoat peaking below the hem of her skirt, busy dusting the panelling and it seemed that Greenwood had found what he was looking for. "Ah!" he intoned with satisfaction. "Miss Pembroke! You will do nicely."

The young lady in question span around at the sound of Greenwood's voice and the colour drained from her face. There were few sights more guaranteed to instil instant fear in a young maid at Castlebridge Hall than that of its majestic butler bearing down on one and carrying a long cane in his right hand. "P...please sir?" she quavered in inquiry.

Greenwood regarded her sternly for a second or two. "May I ask when was the last time you were caned Miss Pembroke?"

The young girl paled even more and swallowed the bile that threatened to rise up in the back of her throat. "P...please sir it were January... just after New Year sir. I...I 'ad fifty strokes in t' library."

Greenwood raised his eyebrows and clucked his tongue in self admonition. "Six months indeed! Dear me! So long! I fear I have been most remiss in my duty." Greenwood turned to his young colleague. "Allow me to introduce you Mr Fletcher. This young lady is Miss Penelope Pembroke. Miss Pembroke is, I'm afraid to say, a young lady with a long history of misbehaviour and a poor disciplinary record. She is just the sort of case that His Lordship has in mind when extolling the virtues of regular beatings. I should most properly have her caned quarterly and it is most negligent of me that I have not attended to her needs since January. I was vaguely aware that it had been some time since her last caning but I had quite forgotten that it had been so long. I was reminded, to some extent, by our head of housekeeping, Mrs Moorhouse, who informed me, just two days ago, that she has had cause to take the strap to the young lady twice within the past month. I was rather busy at the time and unable to attend to her but I did make a mental note to myself to have her to the library for a sound caning when I returned from Scotland. However it is fortuitous that we have encountered her now and she will provide an admirable subject by which to instruct you in the correct deployment of the cane."

Penelope listened to this speech in growing horror. "Am... am I gerrin' t' cane sir?" she asked in a barely audible whisper.

Greenwood nodded gravely. "I'm afraid so Miss Pembroke and, judging by Mrs Moorhouse's remarks concerning your recent conduct, not before time too. However you may at least be relieved that it is to be merely a moderate caning. Had your overdue punishment been further delayed until my return from leave, then it was my intention to have you over the caning stool in the library for a full formal caning of fifty strokes." Greenwood nodded at his companion. "You have Mr Fletcher here to thank for your reprieve. Mr Fletcher will be replacing me during my absence and, since he has little experience in the administration of a disciplinary caning, then you will do most conveniently as a test case to hone his skills on." Greenwood lifted a finger in warning. "Do not, however, for one moment, take my leniency to be a licence for continued misconduct. Those fifty strokes in the library still remain an option Miss Pembroke. I shall ask Mr Fletcher here to keep a close eye on you during my leave and, should he report to me on my return that your conduct and performance has been less than satisfactory, then it will be straight to the library with you and a good hard caning to teach you the error of your ways!"

Penelope bit her lip and looked close to tears. "But I 'aven't done owt wrong sir!"

"That is irrelevant Miss Pembroke and, in any case, I find the veracity of your protestation scarcely credible. Now, if you would be so kind, I would be grateful if you would assume the correct position and present yourself for punishment. Please ensure that your deportment conforms to the mandatory standard Miss Pembroke so as to show a good example to Mr Fletcher here."

"Y...yes sir." whimpered the miserable girl before raising her skirt and petticoat, lowering her knickers and bending over to touch her toes.

Greenwood eyed her critically for a second or two before nodding in approval. "Excellent." he remarked before turning to his younger companion. "Please observe Mr Fletcher the correct deportment for punishment as demonstrated by this young lady here. The feet and legs are kept together and the legs are to be kept straight at all times with no bending at the knee. The young lady is obliged to bend forward at the waist as far as she can without bending her knees; preferably to touch her toes with her fingertips, if she is supple enough at the waist to do so. All the young ladies here at the Hall are taught the correct manner to present themselves for the cane so, under no circumstances, accept any excuse that they were ignorant of the correct stance."

The young man was blushing slightly as he regarded Penelope, obediently presented and awaiting her caning. "Yes sir." he breathed in a hoarse voice.

"You will note also," Greenwood continued "the correct arrangement of her garments. Unless informed to the contrary, any young lady here, upon being informed that she is to be caned and ordered to present herself, is taught to automatically assume that she is to be caned on the bare bottom. Therefore she is expected to raise her skirt and petticoat above her waist and lower her knickers. You are neither expected to have to uncover her bottom for her nor should you need to have to order her to do so. She should perform these functions for you without being asked. It is intended to be humiliating and it is important that the miscreant be expected to participate actively in their own punishment in this way. By doing so they are, in all humility, conceding their culpability and, by affording such assistance to the person punishing them, it is, in effect, a tacit acknowledgement that they deserve their punishment."

Greenwood pointed at the young maid's undergarments. "You will notice the position of the young lady's knickers too Mr Fletcher. Knickers are expected to be lowered at least to the knees. The caning is not confined to the buttocks here at Castlebridge Hall. Both His Lordship and myself are firm exponents of the proposition that the cane should also be delivered to the back of the thighs." Greenwood tapped his cane lightly against the fleshy upper part of Penelope's thighs. "These regions here," he explained, "are most sensitive and a few good hard strokes across the back of the thighs are most effective in teaching the malefactor a salutary lesson that she will not forget in a hurry. For this reason, the knickers must be lowered completely, at least down to the knees, in order to allow full access for the cane to the thighs."

Mr Fletcher nodded eagerly. "I see sir."

"Oh, and while we are discussing the young lady's knickers," Greenwood stated as an afterthought, "You might wish to take a closer look at the pair she is wearing. All the young ladies at the Hall are issued with standard underwear to be worn with their maid's uniforms. They are obliged to wear silk chemise and matching French knickers at all times when on duty; a standing order which I am pleased to see that this young lady is in compliance with. Any other under garments are strictly forbidden and non compliance with this order is to receive a mandatory punishment of at least ten strokes of the cane or thirty strokes of the strap. In the normal course of events, the responsibility for ensuring the correct dress in the matter of undergarments would devolve on Mrs Moorhouse or her head maids. It is they that have the duty to perform regular underwear inspections to ensure conformity to this regulation and it is generally more appropriate to leave such inspections to them unless you have firm grounds to believe that there may be a flagrant transgression of the rule. There may be, however, occasions, such as these, when a young lady is to be punished, when you will have to opportunity to inspect her underwear and ensure that it conforms to the rules. If you discover, on such occasions, that the young lady is wearing anything other than the regulation knickers then you are authorised to add ten strokes of the cane to her sentence and to confiscate the offending undergarment. Is that all clear Mr Fletcher?"

"Yes sir. Crystal clear."

"Excellent!" Greenwood swept a hand over the trembling young figure of Penelope Pembroke still waiting for her caning to begin. "This then," he concluded, "is the correct manner in which the young lady is to present herself. She will be expected to maintain the position throughout her caning. She is forbidden to move, attempt to flinch out of the way of the cane, bend at the knees or rub her bottom. A certain amount of squirming between strokes is unavoidable but any serious failure to maintain the position is to be penalised with extra strokes. Normally I award two strokes for a first offence, four for a second, six for a third and so forth but I leave that to your discretion. Other than a small amount of wriggling, as an unavoidable consequence of the pain of the caning, she must maintain her deportment at all costs and must, under no circumstances, straighten up from her bent over position until given express permission to do so."

"Yes sir." intoned Mr Fletcher even as he wondered just how long the girl could hold that position. She looked a lithe young thing to be sure but the position looked anything but comfortable and he guessed that it must be purgatory for the poor girl to hold still for so long as Mr Greenwood conducted his lecture.

It seemed that Greenwood himself had decided that young Penelope had waited long enough for her caning to commence, for he became suddenly business like and flexed the cane in his hand. "Well now to business!" he declared before removing his jacket and draping it over the back of a chair against the wall. "Perhaps you would care to place your jacket over here as well Mr Fletcher." he offered considerately. "Some flexibility is allowed in the manner of dress when administering punishment as a jacket is somewhat of an encumbrance to a good swing and it is too warm, in any case, for a jacket when engaged in physical labour."

"Yes... thank you sir." said Mr Fletcher, removing his jacket gratefully.

Greenwood rolled up the sleeve of his shirt and swung the cane in his hand through the air a couple of times to judge its weight. Penelope, still bent over in servile submission, cringed at the sound of the long cane cutting the air with a loud whoosh and a tiny whimper of fear escaped her lips. “You might care to flex the cane you're holding Mr Fletcher,” advised Greenwood conversationally. “I am fairly confident that it is a sound instrument but the odd cane does develop a flaw. If you bend the cane and hear a cracking sound we shall have to replace it.”

The bemused young man followed the advice. “It... er it seems sound enough sir.”

“Excellent. Now perhaps you might care to try a couple of practice swings before we commence proceedings... just to familiarise yourself with the implement you understand.”

“Yes of course sir.” Mr Fletcher's practice swings were more enthusiastic than skilful but the sibilant whoosh they produced elicited more whimpers from the cringing Penelope who shuddered with mounting trepidation, her buttocks clenching in involuntary reaction to each sweep of the cane through the air.

Greenwood was watching his younger colleague thoughtfully. “I observe Mr Fletcher that you appear to be left handed. Am I correct?”

“Yes sir. I'm a southpaw I'm afraid. Er...is that a problem.”

“Not a bit of it! On the contrary. It gives me a good idea as to how we may best proceed. If you would care to take up a position to the right of the young lady, while I take up a stance to her left, then we can apply the strokes in alternation from each side. In that way you will be able to follow my lead, as it were, without the necessity of our having to change position continually.”

"Yes sir."

"Good. Now if you assume a stance approximately level with the young lady's hips directly opposite myself." Greenwood placed his cane gently across Penelope's buttocks. The miserable young girl flinched at the cool contact. "You will now have to measure the distance Mr Fletcher," continued Greenwood dispassionately. "Place your cane on the target and take a step back until your arm is nearly at full extension. Keep your back straight. Ideally the final third of the cane should lay fully across the bottom at the end of the swing. Remember that it is the last third of the cane that causes the maximum effect. If you stand too close to your subject then you will strike with the middle of the cane, effectively shortening it, and lose a considerable amount of the impact."

The young man adjusted his stance, observing with interest the perceptible shudder that passed through the young maid at the touch of his cane on her unprotected flesh. "Is that about right sir?"

"Nearly Mr Fletcher. Perhaps just a few inches back however. That's better. Now, if you will allow me, I shall demonstrate a stroke." Greenwood measure the distance once more and raised his arm. "You will note Mr Fletcher that the cane is raised above the shoulder. The stroke is applied with a full swing of the arm from the shoulder. You should avoid strokes from the elbow or flicks of the wrist although, with experience, keeping the arm slightly bent in the opposite direction to the line of swing and straightening it out at the last instance before impact is a technique to be mastered as it increases the speed of the cane as it meets the target." Greenwood remained for a few seconds with the cane poised ominously high above the trembling buttocks of the wretched Penelope. "It is my custom Mr Fletcher," Greenwood explained, "to allow a longish pause before applying the first stroke. This prolonged pause increases the anxiety in the miscreant and serves to augment the punitive effect. Once you have decided that you have kept her on tenterhooks long enough then the stroke should be applied with firm authority. Allow me to demonstrate."

With that, Greenwood swung the cane through the air, with a dreadful whoosh, to strike directly across the centre of Penelope's bottom with a fearful crack. Penelope jerked violently under the impact, threw her head up and let vent to a loud wail of anguish. "You will see," continued Greenwood with his instructions, "That the stroke lands firmly and squarely with solid authority. You should not pull a stroke or bounce it from the target. It should land firm and with force behind it."

Greenwood removed his cane and used the tip of it to point to the point of contact of the first stroke. A white line showed where the cane had landed and, even as Mr Fletcher watched, the line turned to a livid crimson streak transecting the two orbs of Penelope's bottom. "This is the result you are trying to achieve." Greenwood explained. "The cane should leave a clear red stripe, rather resembling a pair of tramlines. Note that the mark extends across both buttocks and, as far as possible, is applied parallel to the ground. Now perhaps you would care to try your arm."

Mr Fletcher swallowed hastily. "Yes sir."

Greenwood watched carefully as the young man measured up his stroke, raised the cane and brought it down across Penelope's bottom. The young girl drew in her breath in a sharp hiss as the cane landed but Greenwood frowned. "It was not *too* bad for a first effort Mr Fletcher but you really need to put a bit more weight behind it." He pointed at Penelope's rear. "If you compare the two marks you'll see that yours is only rather faint and indistinct compared with the far clearer and brighter mark of my first stroke. The sharpness and hue of a cane mark is concomitant with the pain it inflicts and a well defined, deep red stripe is indicative that you are applying yourself with sufficient industry to the task of correcting the subject in question. Allow me to show you once more."

Greenwood wielded the cane in a long, sweeping arc and the pistol like crack of its contact drew a correspondingly sharp squeal from its suffering victim. Greenwood lowered his cane to observe his handiwork. "Now do you see the difference Mr Fletcher?"

The young man leaned forward to peer at the scarlet streak appearing across the still squirming buttocks. "Yes sir. The contrast is marked."

"Well have another try and, if I might be so bold as to say, put a bit more effort into it this time. Don't spare the young lady. She is being taught a lesson after all and we shall do her no favours by stinting on the delivery of that lesson."

"Yes sir." Determined to apply himself with more

credit, Mr Fletcher swung the cane with greater force and was rewarded for his effort with an anguished squeak from the young maid.

Greenwood nodded. "Somewhat better." he allowed. "However it could still do to be a bit harder yet. I find it helps to aim at an imaginary point a short distance beyond the actual point of impact. That way you ensure that the cane lands firmly, with sufficient follow through." To illustrate his point, Greenwood swept the cane down once more, striking with agonising weight into the soft flesh of the lower buttocks. Penelope threw back her head and screamed at the top of her voice as the unbearable flash of pain exploded in her rear.

Greenwood grunted in satisfaction. "That, Mr Fletcher, is a well delivered stroke and, we can tell by the young lady's reaction to it, appears to be having the desired effect. Now try again and let's see if you can't achieve an equally satisfactory result."

This time Mr Fletcher resolved to demonstrate due diligence and application. He adjusted his stance slightly, lifted the cane high above his shoulder and brought it down with as much force as he could muster. Penelope jerked convulsively and howled anew at the latest outrage searing into her buttocks.

"Much, much better!" conceded Greenwood in warm praise. "You can discern from the young lady's vocalisation that she felt that one!"

"Er... is it normal that the young ladies cry out so loudly while being punished sir?" inquired Mr Fletcher tentatively.

Greenwood inclined his head thoughtfully. "Well it varies of course. Some girls are naturally louder than others. Nevertheless it is to be desired that there is a sufficiently vociferous reaction to the caning. You may judge the effectiveness of your corrective measures by the volume and duration of the miscreant's caterwauling. If the young lady in question does not give vent to her feelings with proportionately satisfactory shrieks and yells then you may conclude that the punishment is not having the desired effect and you would be well advised to increase the severity of the strokes."

Greenwood paused to raise a finger of warning counsel. "On the converse side however, there are some young ladies, the more sly and duplicitous among them, who will scream their heads off at the merest touch of the cane with a view to creating the illusion that it is hurting far more than is actually the case. The less experienced, such as yourself, may be taken in by such theatrics and thus fail to apply the cane with sufficient authority or, even, lessen the severity employed. This is something that can only really be learned with experience. I have had the regrettable duty of caning many young ladies in the course of my career and I am not easily misled by such chicanery. If I judge that a young lady is faking I will increase the severity and number of strokes to punish her for her deceitfulness. It is, as I say however, a matter of experience. Doubtless, in due course, once you have a few more canings under your belt, you will learn to distinguish between genuine cries of affliction and mere play acting. Until that time I would advise you to ensure that you apply the cane forcefully, irrespective of the young lady's vocal reactions to it."

"Very well sir."

"Good. Well, now that you seem to have found sufficient swing in your arm, shall we continue? I suggest that we each administer two good hard strokes apiece just to make sure that you have the rhythm as it were."

"As you wish sir."

"Excellent." The broad gallery reverberated with Penelope's screams as the two men applied their canes with exemplary impetus to her tormented rear. At the conclusion of the four strokes Greenwood professed himself satisfied. "Good. You appear to be er... getting into the swing of things Mr Fletcher, if you'll pardon the expression. The young lady's bottom is looking better already. Just one point I would like to make. Do not follow one of my strokes too quickly with one of your own. Allow time for each stroke to sink in. The young lady should be afforded a sufficient period to absorb the lesson of each stroke before the next is applied."

"Very good sir."

"Good. Well now, since you appear to have achieved sufficient power in your swing, I suggest we now work upon your accuracy. We try to achieve an even covering of stripes across the entire bottom and that no area is left untouched." Greenwood tapped his cane on an unmarked space of Penelope's buttocks. "You see this gap here? I am going to land a stroke precisely on this line. Observe."

Greenwood was as good as his word and the

cane cut into the hitherto unsullied region with commendable precision, wrenching another ululating wail from the miserable young Penelope. Greenwood indicated another clear line for his younger colleague's benefit. "Now see if you can land a stroke just here. Fix your eyes on the point you wish to strike and keep them there while you execute the stroke. Make sure that you maintain the necessary force however. Do not sacrifice the strength of the stroke for the sake of accuracy."

"I shall do my best sir."

Although the stroke elicited another scream from Penelope, Greenwood seemed less than impressed by it. "Well the force of the stroke was satisfactory Mr Fletcher but I'm afraid your aim was a little wayward. See here now. Place the cane firmly on the point you wish to strike before drawing back to commence your swing thus. Now keep your eyes glued to the spot as you raise the cane and try to bring it back along exactly the same arc to land just where you had it a second or two before." Greenwood demonstrated once more with another scything stroke. Deafening his ears to Penelope's heart rending wails, he pointed to another portion of the woeful girl's rear. "Now place your cane there and try to achieve a more accurate placement."

Mr Fletcher bit his lip and focussed his concentration. His effort resulted in a much more creditable degree of exactitude and Greenwood seemed pleased. "That's better Mr Fletcher." he declared. "Now in our zeal to achieve a greater perfection of swing and accuracy on the buttocks we have been negligently forgetting to cane the backs of this young lady's thighs. Some strokes across the thighs are a necessary component of her punishment and we mustn't neglect to address them. Now, if you watch closely, you will see just how effective the cane is when applied to these regions."

The cane landed with a fearful meaty smack into the soft fleshy skin close to the top of Penelope's thighs. Penelope's screams exceeded all her earlier efforts and she buckled at the knees under the excruciating agony of the stroke. Greenwood frowned at her. "Please maintain your position Miss Pembroke." he commanded her.

"I...I'm sorry sir." moaned the young girl. "It... it 'urts!"

"I am gratified to hear it young lady. You are being punished and I would be derelict in my duty if it did *not* hurt!" Greenwood turned once again to his colleague. "As you can see Mr Fletcher, the region of the back of the thighs is most sensitive and a stroke there is correspondingly more painful. Would you care to try your hand at one as well?"

"I shall endeavour to do so sir."

Mr Fletcher's cane landed with laudable authority and accuracy across Penelope's thighs, an inch below Greenwood's earlier effort. Penelope screamed long and hard, her shrieks reaching ear-splitting intensity and dwindling away to pathetic sobs as the dampness rolled down the cheeks of her contorted and woeful, face. "Excellent!" declared Greenwood in admiration. "A most meritorious effort, if I may say so, Mr Fletcher. We shall make a disciplinarian out of you yet."

"Thank you sir. It is kind of you to say so."

"Not at all! I see too that you have managed to extract a few tears from our young subject as well."

Is that usual sir?"

"Oh yes. Some girls cry quite easily during punishment of course. Others, more stoic or tougher young ladies, will endure much more before succumbing to tears. It is always a result to be aspired to however. I always feel that some tears are the most reliable indication that the lesson is being well learned, the miscreant's misconduct is being thoroughly rued and that hopefully it will not be a lesson that will be necessary to repeat. I am invariably gratified to see a few tears therefore."

"I see sir."

"Anyway, I'd like you to pay attention to this next stroke." Greenwood placed his cane at the very top of Penelope's thighs, laying it carefully across the crease separating her upper thighs from her buttocks. "This area here," he explained, "is possibly the most sensitive of all. A well delivered stroke here is extremely painful and, for this reason, I usually make a point of delivering the odd one or two to this region. It is, as you will observe, most effective."

Greenwood was not exaggerating. Penelope's blood curdling scream, as he landed the cane with unerring accuracy into the chosen spot, would have quailed the most imperturbable of hearts and once again she collapsed at the knees, unable to hold her stance under the shocking pain. Greenwood looked disappointed in her. "Please maintain your position Miss Pembroke!" he reminded her sternly once more. "I shall not warn you again."

"I... I'm sorry sir." the distressed girl whimpered through her tears.

"Now Mr Fletcher," said Greenwood, returning to address his colleague, "I would like you to try and land your next stroke in the same place. It's perhaps a more difficult stroke to execute but it is a useful skill for you to try to acquire."

"As you wish sir."

Mr Fletcher appeared to be improving by the minute, for his stroke, while not in precisely the same spot, was as close as made little difference. It was too much for poor Penelope. She howled maniacally and fell to her knees, clutching at the tortured flesh at the top of her thighs. Greenwood glared at her. "Disgraceful!" he declared.

Mr Fletcher, believing for a moment that the exclamation referred to his effort, looked chagrined. "I... I'm sorry sir."

Greenwood dismissed his apology out of hand. "No, no Mr Fletcher. I was not addressing you. Your stroke was perfectly in order. It is this young lady who is letting us down for the moment. Very well Miss Pembroke! You have had warnings enough. You will receive two extra strokes! Now resume your position this instance." Weeping piteously, Penelope complied, bending over once more to receive the cane. "I apologise for the young lady's lamentable disobedience Mr Fletcher." said Greenwood gravely. "Perhaps you will allow me to chastise her with the extra two strokes before we continue your instruction."

"Do carry on sir."

"Thank you Mr Fletcher." Greenwood raised his

cane. "Now hold still young lady. The next occasion I am compelled to take you to task for failing to hold your position it will be *four* extra strokes!" To punish her for her failure to maintain her deportment, Greenwood laid the two extra strokes with particular emphasis across the back of her thighs. A fanciful person might have half imagined the stern faces in the portraits, lining the walls of the gallery, raising their eyebrows in surprise at the torrent of demented shrieks the strokes precipitated.

"Now where were we?" asked Greenwood as Penelope's cries descended into heaving sobs. "I think we shall return to the buttocks now shall we. I suggest two more strokes each across the buttocks and then another stoke apiece across the thighs and we can review your performance then Mr Fletcher."

"Very well sir."

The six strokes proceeded accordingly and Penelope, having no desire to earn herself further penalty strokes, held her position admirably, confining herself to loud screams of dismay and to tossing her head from side to side in agony." Greenwood was impressed with his younger colleague's progress and, at the conclusion of the six strokes, leaned forward to examine Penelope's rump critically. The anguished girl's rear was displaying a most satisfactory lattice work of angry red stripes. "Well Mr Fletcher," Greenwood declared, "I must say that you seem to be taking to the task like a duck to water. Very commendable!"

"Thank you sir."

"Well merited young man. Now let me see. If my memory is not deceiving me, I make that twenty strokes, not counting the two extras, that Miss Pembroke here has received. I propose therefore, now you have your eye in as it were, that we finish the job with a final five strokes each. That will, assuming that Miss Pembroke does not procure any further extra strokes for herself, bring the tally up to a total of thirty as well as the two extras she has already received. Ready for one last effort?"

"Yes sir."

"Good man! Let us proceed." The final ten strokes were a bitter torment for the hapless young maid as she screamed herself hoarse under the assault of the canes. Her pinched red face was wet with tears, that rolled down her cheeks and even trickled down to form drops on the end of her nose. Finally, at the very end of the limits of her endurance, the awful caning ceased. Greenwood stepped back to observe the results. The swollen orbs and thighs, with their vivid scarlet stripes, seemed almost to pulsate gently in the sunlight filtering through the gallery windows. "Now that Mr Fletcher," declared Greenwood in satisfaction, "is, albeit not a pleasant one, a job well done!

Mr Fletcher, stepping around to observe Penelope's heavily striped bottom more closely, could only partially agree with Greenwood's analysis. It was true, he would concede, that Penelope's bottom had been most satisfactorily caned but he could not concur with his superior's assertion that the task of caning it had been a disagreeable one. In fact, although it would not do to show it, he had enjoyed the exercise very much indeed. He was looking forward to his sojourn as

Mr Greenwood's locum at the Hall and hoped very much to have the opportunity to hone his newly acquired skills on some more of the Hall's personable young maids. "Yes sir." he answered, keeping his voice as neutral as possible. "It would appear that Miss Pembroke here has been suitably chastised."

"I quite agree Mr Fletcher," concurred Greenwood "and, regrettable though the necessity may be, we may at least congratulate ourselves on having discharged our duty to the best of our ability."

"Er... quite so sir."

"You may stand up straight now Miss Pembroke." Greenwood informed the young maid.

Penelope complied, still weeping miserably. To Mr Fletcher's surprise, Penelope made no effort to readjust her dress and held her skirt and petticoat high above her waist. Nor did she make any attempt to recover her knickers which had slipped from her knees, during the course of her caning, and come to reside in a crumpled heap about her ankles. Instead, still holding up her skirt and petticoat she shuffled around to face her two caners. She took a moment or two to compose herself before addressing them in a suitably meek and contrite voice. "Thank you fer givin' me the punishment wot I deserved sirs." she intoned in rehearsed speech, "I'm sorry for my disgraceful misconduct and I promise faithfully ter be'ave better in future."

Mr Fletcher blinked in surprise at this extraordinary declaration and turned to look at Greenwood inquiringly.

"It is a mandatory requirement Mr Fletcher." Greenwood explained. "Following punishment, the young lady is not allowed to readjust her attire until she has thanked you for taking the trouble to punish her, apologised for her misbehaviour and given assurances that it will not recur in the future."

"Oh! I see."

"Having done so, she will then wait until you indicate that you are satisfied with her contrition and grant her permission to clothe herself decently once more. Following a formal caning in the library she would be expected to spend half an hour kneeling on a hard wooden bench with skirts raised, knickers down and her hands on her head to fully absorb the lesson but that is not particularly practicable for less formal punishments, delivered elsewhere in the Hall, and where a period of penance would keep the young lady from her duties. It is therefore perfectly acceptable, assuming that you are convinced that she has learned her lesson properly, to merely deliver a stern warning concerning her future conduct, grant her permission to re-clothe herself and dismiss her to be about her duty."

Greenwood paused to rub his chin thoughtfully. "There is one, somewhat delicate, matter I need to tell you about before we allow Miss Pembroke here to cover her modesty. At the risk of embarrassing you Mr Fletcher, may I draw your attention to the young lady's private parts. You will see that they are devoid of pubic hairs. I realise that this is a little unsavoury but you should be aware that Lord Castlebridge is a great stickler for this. It is his opinion that a bush of pubic hair is both unsightly and unhygienic on a young lady and therefore insists that all the girls at the Hall keep themselves cleanly shaven in that region. It is perhaps rather an unusual requirement to expect the young ladies to adhere to but His Lordship is most resolute in the matter and, since he is the master of this house and we are duty bound to obey his wishes, it is a strictly enforced regulation. Now usually, in the normal course of events, this is a regulation more properly controlled by the senior female members of the household who are authorised to conduct spot inspections on their charges to ensure that it is adhered to. They are also the ones who normally apply the mandatory punishment for this offence which, I understand to be, is a whipping with the martinet in the offending region between the legs. So normally you would not be expected to concern yourself with this matter. The exception however is during those times when you are called upon to punish one of the young ladies for some other matter. If the young lady, upon lowering her knickers for the cane, reveals that she is in transgression of this regulation then you are, by standing order of His Lordship himself, obliged to award her an extra ten strokes of the cane and also to report the matter to the senior female in her department so that she may, at her discretion, apply the mandatory punishment as well."

"I see sir." the young Mr Fletcher ran a finger under the collar of his shirt. He seemed to be becoming rather heated; a condition not entirely ascribable to the torrid summer heat.

Greenwood turned his attention to the still snivelling Penelope. “Very well Miss Pembroke. I shall accept for the moment your assurances of improvement in your behaviour. Be aware however that there are still fifty strokes of the cane hanging over you in the library. I shall be asking Mr Fletcher here to monitor your conduct closely during my absence and you would be well advised to ensure that it remains impeccable. If Mr Fletcher reports to me, on my return, that it has been anything but, then be assured that you will be straight along to the library to face the caning stool. Do I make myself clear?”

Penelope quivered her bottom lip abjectly and nodded her head. “Y... yes sir.”

“Very well. In that case you may pull up your knickers, adjust your dress and you are dismissed.”

“Th... thank you sir.” Penelope hastily restored her modesty, picked up her work materials and tottered off down the gallery with the peculiarly stiff legged gait of a girl who has just suffered more than thirty hard strokes of the cane.

Greenwood glanced at his watch. “Well I see that the afternoon is well advanced. His Lordship will be returning home soon and I have some chores to perform so if there are no further questions...”

Mr Fletcher shook his head. “No I think you've covered most of my queries sir. I must be leaving shortly in any case or I shall miss the bus from the village. I'd like to thank you for all the trouble you've gone to in instructing me this afternoon.”

“It was entirely my pleasure Mr Fletcher. Indeed it is I who should thank you for coming along at such short notice to cover my absence. If any further questions occur to you before next week please feel free to telephone me here."

"Thank you sir. I shall do"

Greenwood held out his hand. "In that case I shall take my leave of you Mr Fletcher. I will, circumstances allowing, most likely see you briefly on your arrival the day of my departure. If I do not, for some reason, then allow me to wish you the very best of luck."

"Thank you sir."

The two men shook hands and parted amiably. Mr Fletcher scurried off in search of the servant's exit from the Hall and the walk back to the village. Greenwood returned to his pantry. He had been slightly less than candid with his junior colleague. Lord Castlebridge was not due home for an hour at least and there were no really pressing matters to attend to until dinner time. Instructing junior butlers was thirsty work in this weather however and he had a mind to take an hour of ease over another mug of cool beer. He hoped that there would be nothing more of a tasking nature for the rest of the day and he particularly hoped that the young ladies of Castlebridge Hall would behave themselves for the evening and thus preclude him from having the chore of correcting them. It was a futile hope. Greenwood did not know it yet, but his disciplinary duties for the day were far from over.

CHAPTER 5

"How much did you say?" demanded Lord Castlebridge in outrage. Lady Castlebridge flushed, lowered her head miserably and repeated the amount in a barely audible murmur. His Lordship glared at his wife. It would be true to say that he was not in the best of humours. He had returned home from the city office in a most irascible temper. There were several irritating matters in his business dealings, of intractable nature, demanding his attention quite apart from a particular catastrophe perpetrated by his junior executive's damn foolish wife. Then there were a number of domestic headaches that were proving infuriating. Neither was the weather alleviating his ill humour on that score.

The unseasonal June heat wave, that had lasted fully three weeks now, had brought a new problem, for his tenant farmers' were pleading with him for assistance for their parched crops. The Hall was under drought restrictions too and the head gardener, unable to use the sprinklers, was viewing the arid stubble, of what had once been the verdant green lawns in front of Castlebridge Hall, with something close to desperation. The stifling heat had exacerbated everybody's tempers and it was intolerably muggy even with all the windows open in the Hall. He had thought of having air conditioning installed but it had seemed an unnecessary expense for the three or four weeks of the year that the capricious English climate would actually justify its existence.

Now, to top it all, he was faced with this; his wife's effrontery to come along to him here in his study and meekly inform him that she had somehow contrived to lose seven thousand pounds of the household budget on the bloody horses at Royal Ascot the weekend before! Seven thousand pounds! He couldn't imagine what she'd been thinking about!

His wife was an enthusiastic attendee at the higher class race meetings but they had generally tended to be more social events than anything else; a chance to meet her socialite friends and parade in her finery around the paddocks, basking under the approving observation of her gentleman admirers. She was apt to wager on the races of course. She had an unerring eye for the horses. She would invariably pick out the one horse whose worth was of better value at a glue factory than gracing a race track! He couldn't remember the last time she had actually picked out a winner. Last year, for instance, she had eagerly laid down two hundred pounds on some wretched gelding which had proved so slow that His Lordship had acidly remarked that, but for a last minute burst of speed in the final two furlongs, would have been in grave danger of becoming mixed up in the next race!

Nevertheless he had tolerated his wife's indulgence until now for she enjoyed enormously the social life at the racetrack and, if she had invariably lost money, had hitherto restricted that loss to within acceptable limits. It seemed however that, at Ascot, she must have been gripped by some temporary insanity and thrown all caution to the wind! Seven thousand pounds! She must have been mad! And that wasn't an end to it either Lord Castlebridge thought to himself sourly. If you added all the new dresses, shoes and hats and she'd purchased for Ascot this year you could easily round that up to over five figures!

Of course, had Lord Castlebridge but known it, the figure was already well into five figures. Lady Castlebridge had not entirely spent the afternoon playing with her maids. She had indulged in a little creative book-keeping as well; managing to bury some five thousand pounds of the Ascot debacle beneath an obfuscating morass of "household expenses" in the hope that seven thousand, as opposed to twelve, would somehow seem a more tolerable deficiency for her husband to swallow. With this optimistic view, she had sought out her husband, on his return to the Hall, and meekly confessed to this amended profligacy to pre-empt his hearing of it from other sources. Hopefully, her husband would be impressed with her honesty and contrition and she might yet escape with a little blustering and a stern lecture on the imperatives of prudence and frugality. It wasn't much of a hope, Lady Castlebridge admitted to herself, but it was the best she had.

It was shaping up to be a forlorn hope indeed. Her purely cosmetic tinkering and affected humility had seemingly done little to mollify her husband's ill temper. Lord Castlebridge, already with enough headaches on his plate, was in no mood, perceptibly inclined towards charity and forgiveness. In the current economic climate, when he was forever preaching the virtues of austerity and cost cutting, the last thing he needed was his wife to suddenly take leave of her senses and start throwing money away like water!

She was shuffling her feet uncomfortably on the carpet her face pink with embarrassed contrition. He glared at exasperatedly. She wasn't, he had to admit, a deliberately wilful woman. On the contrary she was generally admirably respectful, mostly obedient and, at twelve years his junior, a highly attractive young woman whose peachy complexion, soft curvaceous figure and luxurious, wavy blond hair had made her the toast of half the young studs in the county. She was, all told, a most admirable adornment to the hallowed portals of Castlebridge Hall and His Lordship, although apt these days to seek out his sexual gratification away from the trappings of matrimony, was still fond of her.

If she had a fault, in Lord Castlebridge's opinion, it was that she was too easily led into foolishness by the wayward young ladies of her social acquaintance. Lord Castlebridge suspected that the weekend's rashness could well be attributed to this failing. There were several young ladies within his wife's social circles of whom he disapproved and of whom he privately considered it to be a lamentable fact that their husbands had not the strength of character to take a firmer hand with. Not least among this particular circle, of course, was the wife of his junior executive, young Roger Brideshead, whose folly he had been trying to repair for the last two days and whose misbehaviour might have brought ruin down on all of them.

Lord Castlebridge shook his head to clear it of that particular problem and turned instead to the matter in hand. He was a wealthy man and, in the greater scheme of things, seven thousand pounds hardly amounted to a catastrophe. But he considered it to be the thin edge of the wedge. He could hardly ask his household to make cutbacks in times of economic austerity whilst his own wife set such a poor example with her profligate spending. Furthermore there was a darker side to her foolishness. Lord Castlebridge was all too aware of the destructive nature of compulsive gambling behaviour. The occasional modest wager was all well and good but this sort of thing needed to be nipped in the bud.

Well fortunately this was one problem, among the many demanding his attention at the moment, that could be dealt with swiftly and efficiently. In quick decision he rang the service bell behind his desk before turning his attention back to his wife. "Well this just isn't good enough Cynthia!" he told her sternly. "I can't think what the blazes got into you!"

Lady Castlebridge's lowered her eyes abjectly and quivered her lip pathetically. "I'm sorry Rupert." she murmured in a soft voice, still hoping against hope to appease her clearly irritated husband.

"Yes well not as sorry as you're going to be madam! I'll not have this sort of thing do you hear? What kind of example are you setting to the rest of the household by squandering money in this fashion? It's not as if you had the remotest chance of winning anything on the damn horses after all, given your previous racing form. What the devil possessed you to throw away money like that on some damned nag?"

"I...I'm sorry Rupert." she repeated miserably, "It won't happen again."

"Of that I am quite sure madam!" His Lordship informed her determinedly. "I shall take steps to ensure that it *won't* happen again; firm steps madam!"

Lady Castlebridge shuddered involuntarily, under no illusions about the sort of steps implied in her husband's tone. It was by no means the first time she had incurred his wrath and she was well familiar with the kind of measures he considered appropriate for misconduct on this scale. She resigned herself to the inevitable. She had learned long ago not to argue and that pitiful pleading was futile. She gave a little sob and lowered her eyes. "Yes Rupert." she acknowledged in a croaked whisper.

At this point there was a discreet knock on the study door. "Come in!" barked Lord Castlebridge and the door opened to reveal the solemn and dignified presence of Thomas Greenwood, Castlebridge Hall's majestic butler.

"You rang My Lord?"

"Ah there you are Greenwood! Are you busy for the moment? I understand you have that young chap over from Torsbury Towers to show him the ropes before you go swanning off to Scotland."

"The young gentleman was here this afternoon for three hours My Lord but we concluded our business and he has already departed. I understand that he was desirous of catching the five o'clock bus from the village."

"So you're free then?"

"I have a few routine matters to attend to My Lord but nothing of pressing urgency if there was some particular service you required of me."

"I see. Well, in that case, I wonder if you would do me a service."

"Yes My Lord?"

"Yes! My wife here is in need of a good sound caning!"

Greenwood lifted an eyebrow austerely. "Indeed My Lord!" he remarked, ignoring the soft sob that escaped from Her Ladyship's lips. "I am sorry to hear that. In what way has Her Ladyship displeased you if I may be bold enough to ask?"

"Only gone and thrown away seven thousand pounds on some blasted cripple of a horse at Ascot over the weekend!"

"Really My Lord? That was perhaps a little imprudent of Her Ladyship."

"Bloody downright madness is how I would have put it!"

"Certainly Her Ladyship could have possibly exercised better judgement in the matter My Lord."

"Exactly! Well I'd like her to learn to exercise that better judgement in future Greenwood. So, if your duties permit, I'd be grateful if you'd do me the service of marching her straight down to the library and teaching her a salutary lesson with your cane!"

"I shall attend to the matter immediately My

Lord." Greenwood frowned in concern. "There is one small consideration however My Lord. We have workmen in the library this week, effecting some needed repair work on the floors and panelling, and I'm afraid the chamber is in no fit state to be used."

"Damn yes! I'd forgotten about that."

"If I might be permitted to make a suggestion My Lord, I can attend to Her Ladyship's chastisement with equal facility in my pantry. It is perhaps a somewhat more informal setting but it does contain all the accoutrements necessary for the task required. I have had most of the items pertinent to disciplinary functions, including the library caning stool, installed temporarily in my pantry. If you require me to discipline Her Ladyship then I would have everything to hand.

"Capital! Excellent idea Greenwood."

"Thank you My Lord. May I be permitted to inquire the severity of the caning you feel warranted in this instance My Lord?"

Lord Castlebridge pondered for a moment. "I should think fifty strokes should do the trick Greenwood." He glanced sharply at his wife who had gasped audibly as her sentence was pronounced. She was looking pale. Fifty strokes was a severe sentence. It had been nearly eighteen months since Lord Castlebridge had last had her caned and that had only been twenty five strokes which had been ordeal enough. Lady Castlebridge took a deep breath and clasped her hands tightly to still their trembling.

Even Greenwood seemed momentarily taken aback by the severity of the punishment imposed upon Her Ladyship. “Fifty strokes My Lord?” he asked by way of confirmation.

“That’s right Greenwood and I want all of them delivering so mind you keep a careful tally.”

“You may rely on me My Lord. Will Her Ladyship be permitted to retain her undergarments for the duration of her punishment?”

Lord Castlebridge shook his head decisively. “No, no, no Greenwood! The bare bottom if you please. She thoroughly deserves it.”

“As you wish My Lord. I shall carry out your instructions to the letter.”

“Excellent.” Lord Castlebridge raised a finger in admonition. “And make sure you lay them on good and hard Greenwood. Don’t spare her! A good firm hand is what she needs. I want a thorough job doing.”

Greenwood looked mildly offended by the implied suggestion that he might not perform his duty with his customary diligence. “As always, I shall endeavour to provide perfect satisfaction My Lord.” he remarked with just a hint of defensive wounded pride.

“Good! See that you do. I shall be inspecting her backside at dinner and I’ll expect to see that my wishes have been carried out to my satisfaction.”

“You may have no concerns My Lord. Your instructions will be carried out precisely in accordance with your wishes.”

“Capital! Well carry on Greenwood.”

“Yes My Lord.” He turned to the wretched figure of Lord Castlebridge’s wife. “If you would please accompany me My Lady then.” Lady Castlebridge nodded abjectly but she obediently followed the butler out of the door. Lord Castlebridge watched them go in satisfaction. At least his wife had had more sense than to object to the punishment imposed. She had looked terrified, it is true, but she had walked off to her fate with submissive resignation. It was not unusual for His Lordship to ask his butler to cane his wife. Greenwood was the man generally charged with disciplinary duties at Castlebridge Hall and his height, muscular build and strong right arm were eminently suited to the task. Early in their marriage Lord Castlebridge had administered whatever punishments his wife had earned personally but, these days, he was just as likely to delegate the task to Greenwood as not. She was certainly not unfamiliar with the firmness of Castlebridge Hall's butler's right hand!

Lady Castlebridge was reflecting miserably on that very subject herself. Eighteen months before, she had been obliged to receive twenty five strokes of the cane, administered with the full authority of Greenwood's right arm in the library, and it was not an experience she had been in any hurry to repeat. The caning had been agonising and she'd been in pain for days afterwards. The marks on her bottom had been clearly visible a week later! The impression it had left in her mind had lasted a lot longer; sufficiently so to deter her from any risk of a repetition. Now it seemed, as she followed meekly in Thomas Greenwood's wake, she was, not only fated to repeat the experience, but to have it doubled! Her throat felt dry with fear and her legs were trembling uncontrollably.

It was some distance to the pantry for, this part of Castlebridge Hall, formed a hollow square about an inner courtyard and Greenwood's pantry lay on the far side of this courtyard, necessitating a considerable walk around three sides of the Hall, if one did not choose to cut across the central plaza. Inevitably they encountered some of the Hall's considerable retinue of servants on that long, doom laden walk. In due accordance with her penitent status, Lady Castlebridge walked a pace or two behind Greenwood. The significance of this was not lost on the servants they passed. It was certainly evident to the two young chambermaids they encountered in the Long Hall, who winked at each other and giggled behind their hands after the solemn little procession had passed. In the normal course of events, Lady Castlebridge, as mistress of the house, would lead the way with Greenwood respectfully in the rear. But protocol was strictly adhered to at Castlebridge Hall and Her Ladyship trailing behind could only mean one thing; she was on her way to a caning.

News travelled quickly around a place as confined as Castlebridge Hall. It would very quickly be all over the Hall that Her Ladyship was about to be caned. Doubtless many of the servants would neglect their duties to gather in strategic places to catch the sounds or, better yet, the glimpse of their mistress's suffering under the cane. There was nothing particularly personal in this for Lady Castlebridge was kind to her servants and generally well liked. Nevertheless there was always that somewhat subversive thrill among the serving classes when one of their superiors had their comeuppance for once.

At the entrance to his pantry Greenwood opened the door and stepped aside to usher Her Ladyship in politely. “If you please My Lady?” Taking a deep breath, Lady Castlebridge stepped through the ominous portal into the chamber beyond. Greenwood’s pantry was not a room that she was familiar with for it was a peculiarly masculine reserve within the Hall. It was the place where Greenwood was apt to pass his leisure hours in one of the old but comfortable leather armchairs by the big fireplace with a glass of port in his hand from his considerable stock arraigned on shelves about the walls. It was a surprisingly large chamber albeit of somewhat rude stone walls in contrast to the highly polished wooden panelling prevalent throughout the more genteel regions of the hall. The furniture was simple and rather battered but the whole place bespoke an air of masculine comfort; a sort of safe haven into which the men of the house could escape from the more fussy sensibilities of the womenfolk.

It was a place where Greenwood’s cronies among the staff would gather of an evening to chew the fat around the fire whilst making inroads into the Hall’s liquor stocks. The head gardener and the gamekeeper were regular visitors to this cosy sanctuary as was the head chef. Even Lord Castlebridge was apt on occasion to pop in to share a bottle with his butler. But women were very rare visitors here and usually only then under similar circumstances to those currently being experienced by Lady Castlebridge herself.

Stepping into the room, the first item, among the furniture and shelving, Her Ladyship noted was one that brought a further thrill of fear to her. The caning stool was the all too familiar apparatus that normally resided upstairs in the library and of which she had such painful memories. Standing alone in a clear open space it was a high wooden structure with sturdy, straight legs set on a stable platform. The top of the stool was a curved indented surface to accommodate the belly of the victim lying prostrate across it. A thick leather strap with buckles looped over this surface to secure the body of the miscreant to this surface whilst further straps on all four legs served to buckle their legs and wrists.

Lady Castlebridge shuddered. Her last acquaintance with the cane had not involved the caning stool since she had only received twenty five strokes. Now she was facing fifty and would doubtless be secured helplessly to this barbaric contraption. For less severe punishments it was usually merely necessary to bend over and present oneself for the cane but, facing a sentence of fifty strokes, Her Ladyship had little doubt that she would be required to suffer the indignity of being strapped to the caning stool to receive her punishment.

Her heart was beating loudly in her chest. Her hands felt clammy. It was warm in the room in spite of the windows looking out onto the courtyard being open but she felt chilled and shivered. She stood uncertainly in the middle of the room her legs feeling weak beneath her. Greenwood cleared his throat. “I have a few preparations to attend to for your punishment My Lady, if you’ll forgive me. Perhaps in the meantime you would care to be removing your lower undergarments for convenience.”

Lady Castlebridge blinked foolishly. “You... you mean my knickers?”

Greenwood nodded gravely. “Yes My Lady. Your punishment is to be carried out on the bare bottom. His Lordship was most specific in his instructions and I’m afraid I must insist.”

Lady Castlebridge swallowed and bit her lip. “Yes... yes of course.” she whispered dolefully. As she lifted her skirt and petticoat to lower her knickers Greenwood busied himself clearing a few obstructions from the area around the caning stool, removed his jacket to hang it on a peg on the wall and walked over to a slim cabinet which he opened to reveal a selection of canes and leather straps. Lady Castlebridge’s knickers became entangled in the heels of her shoes as she tried to slip them off her feet and she hopped around in an undignified manner for a second or two before finally relieving herself of them. Finally free of the encumbrance around her ankles she stood there foolishly, holding her knickers in her hand, as Greenwood pondered the choice of implements in his cabinet in grave solemnity.

He seemed to take an age in making his choice, rubbing his chin thoughtfully and reaching out to finger the canes hanging on their pegs in the cabinet. At last he made his choice and lifted a cane down lovingly from its hook. Lady Castlebridge quailed at the sight of it; five feet of solid rattan cane, fashioned with a leather grip at one end, a quarter of an inch thick and gleaming evilly in pale yellow before Her Ladyship's horrified eyes. Greenwood flexed the implement experimentally in his hand to assure himself that there were no flaws in the cane and, having ascertained that it was indeed sound, he swished it through the air a couple of times to judge its weight and length. Lady Castlebridge felt her buttocks clench involuntarily at the evil hiss the wicked looking cane made as it swung through the air.

Satisfied with the instrument he had chosen Greenwood turned his attention back to Lady Castlebridge. He saw the pair of knickers she was still holding in her hand. She didn't seem to know what to do with them. He nodded at her dilemma and indicated a small side table near the fire. "Ah yes My Lady. Perhaps you would care to place the garment on the small table over there. It is perfectly clean I assure you." Lady Castlebridge nodded dumbly and placed her knickers on the table indicated. For some reason she felt obliged to neatly fold her knickers before placing them carefully on the table. Greenwood nodded again in satisfaction as she turned back toward him. "Excellent My Lady. I think we may proceed now." He paused for a second before continuing. "In view of the severity of the sentence His Lordship has imposed on you My Lady I think it best that you were restrained for the duration of your punishment."

"Yes Thomas." she whispered feebly in agreement. She was one of the few people in the household who ever used Greenwood's Christian name.

"In that case would you kindly step forward to the stool My Lady?"

Lady Castlebridge obeyed meekly, stepping up onto the box in front of the high stool so that the top of the stool was level with her upper hips. Taking a deep breath to still the whimpers that came to her lips, she bent slowly forward over the stool until she was only touching the box behind with her toes. Desperately she gripped the front legs of the stool in her hands. Greenwood noted her satisfactory position in approval and laid the cane aside for a moment to attend to the fastenings on the stool. "Excuse me My Lady." He apologised politely, as he took the broad leather strap across her waist and buckled it firmly pressing her stomach against the hard wooden surface of the stool. He squatted at the front of the stool and addressed her not unkindly. "If you would give me your hand please My Lady." Lady Castlebridge obeyed and he buckled her left wrist securely to the stool's legs. "And the other if you please." He repeated the process with her right wrist.

Satisfied with his preparations at that end he moved around to her rear. Stretched over the stool, Lady Castlebridge's dress and petticoat had ridden high up her thighs and they were little hindrance to Greenwood as he gently grasped her left leg and lifted it clear of the box to buckle the strap on the back leg of the stool around her stockinged leg just above her knee. Her Ladyship hated this next part for, when he took her other leg, she lost all contact with her feet on the ground and her legs were pulled apart and her feet suspended in the air as he buckled the other leg strap.

Greenwood moved the box, she had stood on to lean over the stool, out of the way and then made a last check of her fastenings to make sure that all were firm and secure, but not cutting off the circulation in any way. He took pride in the meticulousness of his preparations. Finally he moved back to her rear once more. "If you will forgive me My Lady." He intoned as he took the hem of her dress and petticoat and lifted it up to lie across her back exposing her naked buttocks for the cane.

Greenwood frowned at this moment. Her Ladyship was wearing stockings held by garters high on her thighs. They in no way impeded access of the cane to her bottom but they did cover most of the back of her thighs. It was, as Greenwood had explained to the young Mr Fletcher, a rule of thumb in the Hall that the sensitive backs of the thighs were caned in addition to the buttocks during punishment and, when His Lordship had specified that he wished her caned on the bare backside, it was implicit in those instructions that the backs of her thighs were to be caned on the naked flesh as well as her bottom. With this in mind, Greenwood had obviously been less than explicit in his instructions to Her Ladyship, when asking her to remove her undergarments. Technically her stockings were undergarments too and he should have asked her to remove them or at least roll them down to her knees. Now, since she was already secured to the stool, he would have to do it for her.

"Pardon me My Lady but I'm afraid I must roll your stockings down." he told her matter-of-factly. Lady Castlebridge whimpered piteously. The significance of his statement was not wasted on her. She would be caned on the back of her legs in those spots where it hurt the most; the upper thighs. She felt his fingers at the elastic of her garters and then her stockings pulled down to the straps restraining her legs. Her entire rear from the small of her back to just above her knees was now suitable exposed for the cane's attention. She felt the tears pricking at her eyes in fear and her caning had not even begun.

Greenwood stood back and regarded his handiwork critically. Her Ladyship was admirably positioned over the stool, feet clear of the ground and the relevant parts of her anatomy stretched out, pushed up and perfectly presented for the cane. He allowed himself a nod of satisfaction. "I think that should suffice My Lady, so, with your permission, I think we may begin."

Lady Castlebridge nodded helplessly. "Yes Thomas," she snivelled. "You may proceed."

Greenwood nodded once more "Thank you My Lady." Carefully he rolled his shirt sleeve up on his right arm and flexed his arm to loosen up. The he picked up the cane. He took up his stance behind her and measured the distance. "Forgive me My Lady but I'm afraid the strokes will be very hard. His Lordship was most explicit in this regard and I would be failing in my duty if I were not to follow his instructions to the letter."

Lady Castlebridge swallowed feebly. "I quite

understand Thomas." she whispered in a tiny voice.

"In that case My Lady... if you are quite ready."

She could only manage a tiny nod. She stared straight ahead, clenching her teeth and grasping hold of the legs of the stool until her knuckles turned white, as Greenwood lifted the cane high over his shoulder. There was an awful pause. The swish of the cane was loud in the quiet of the room and louder still was the harsh crack as it landed with force into the soft flesh of the centre of her buttocks.

The loud crack of the cane and the accompanying strangled gasp from its recipient was clearly audible across the courtyard to Lord Castlebridge as he stood by the open window of his study looking out thoughtfully. The afternoon was late. He glanced at his watch and noted that there was a little under two hours to go before dinner. Perhaps he should put his worries away for one day and treat himself to a small tumbler of fine malt whisky. There was another crack of the cane and a snort, that sounded as if it had emerged from between clenched teeth, from across the courtyard. He felt a certain pride in that his wife was undoubtedly attempting to suppress her cries under the agony of the cane.

For all her occasional foolishness there was something fundamentally sound about his beautiful wife. He would not have her punished unless he had good reason to and she tacitly accepted the justice of his decisions in this regard and took the punishments that he was occasionally obliged to have ministered to her without protest and with as much dignity as she could muster. It was characteristic that she would try to stifle her cries of pain and take her punishment in dignified silence as befitting her station as the lady of the house.

Of course, Lord Castlebridge realised, it would not last. His wife had a low tolerance for pain and would doubtless lose her ability to control her cries within a few strokes. Well that was no bad thing, he reflected. She was after all being punished and, implicit in that, was a certain loss of dignity. Lord Castlebridge was a great believer in the efficacious, educational effects of humility and considered that occasional lessons in the folly of excess pride to be character building. His wife's humiliation would remain in her mind to teach her the error of her ways long after the throbbing in her bottom had subsided.

He stood and listened to two or three more strokes of the cane and, when its impact finally forced a loud squeal from his wife's lips, he nodded in satisfaction and turned to walk to his drinks cabinet to take a bottle of fine eighteen year old Talisker malt. Lord Castlebridge had a liking for the pungent malt whiskies of the Western Isles. He poured himself a rather generous tumblerful in the event, considering that, after the disagreeable annoyances of the last few days, he had earned it. He swilled the amber liquid around in the glass and sniffed the tangy aroma appreciatively before returning to his place at the open window.

His wife's caning was progressing nicely by the sound of things. Now that she had lost the restraint of her control, she was giving vent to loud shrieks and wails to accompany the harsh crack of the cane across her bare flesh. Well it would be a long time before she thought to squander money on a horse again! He grunted to himself in satisfaction. This was how he liked problems to be solved; sharp, decisively and in the shortest time possible. Many a man would have failed to take such immediate and effective action; allowed his wife's problem to fester and grow into something much more serious. Lord Castlebridge considered himself no such man however. Once confronted with his wife's foolishness he had taken immediate and firm measures. Twenty minutes over the caning stool and he had every confidence that his wife's potential gambling problem would be solved permanently. He wished every problem was as amenable to such a ready solution; Roger Brideshead's foolish wife for instance.

He frowned at the thought and took a sip of his whisky as another shrill squeal of agony echoed around the courtyard. Roger's wife had been a thorn in his side ever since his younger junior had inadvisably married the young filly. Oh he could understand the attraction to Roger because there was no doubt at all that she was as fine a young specimen of womanhood as it would be possible to wish for with long brown hair, a well turned figure and captivating looks. Roger had been smitten from the moment he had cast eyes on her and quite clearly worshipped her.

That was half the problem thought Lord Castlebridge bitterly. Roger was far too enamoured of his wife to take note of her faults and the necessary measures to correct them. He deferred to her wishes far too much; pampered her in fact. He should have laid a firm hand on her the moment he slipped a ring on her finger. But he hadn't. He had let her have her own way for far too long and his lack of control over her was coming back to haunt him. She was a woman that needed a strong hand, it was certain. Had she been His Lordship's wife he would have established the ground rules from the beginning and had her marched along to the library for a sound thrashing on her wedding night!

She wasn't a bad woman as such, Brenda Brideshead, but she was a sadly flawed one in many respects. Her undoubted beauty had led her to a consuming vanity and made her an easy target for flattery as a result. Combine that with her foolishness, her garrulous nature and her reprehensible indiscretion and you had a recipe for disaster. It was too bad of Roger that he had allowed things to get so out of hand.

Lord Castlebridge sighed, an exhalation whose sound was drowned by another piercing shriek from the far side of the courtyard. In the normal course of events he would consider that a married man's private life was his own affair and, whether he disapproved of the way in which a gentleman dealt with his wife or not, it was not his concern to interfere. The trouble was that Brenda Brideshead's actions extended beyond the domain of the domestic hearth and now impacted directly on the dealings of Roger and his own business dealings, and that very much was his concern.

Again Roger himself had to take some blame for this for he was far too open with his wife, concerning business matters, and she was privy to the inner private matters of the business to an extent that Lord Castlebridge found shocking. Certainly His Lordship would never have dreamed of the same degree of confidence in the lady now screaming loudly under the ministrations of Greenwood's cane on the far side of the courtyard. Roger doted on her too much and allowed her too much access to those matters that Lord Castlebridge considered to be the business of gentlemen.

It would not have been so bad, he considered, had she been the sort of woman whose discretion and confidentiality could be relied upon. For all his misogyny, Lord Castlebridge was bound to admit that there were ladies among his acquaintance with whom he could trust his most private matters with the utmost confidence. Brenda Brideshead was not one of them! She was an insatiable socialite whirling from one dinner party, soiree, ball or cocktail party after another. In this social maelstrom of hers she was all too likely, in her foolish excitement, doubtless fuelled by copious amounts of champagne, to lose her head and babble unreservedly. She was particularly prone to loosen her tongue when under the flattering attentions of personable young men. She was an unrepentant flirt and liked nothing more than to be surrounded by admiring gentlemen, often with less than honourable intentions upon her.

Lord Castlebridge frowned at this thought and took another sip of his whisky as a further crack of the cane caused a demented shriek to reverberate about the courtyard. Brenda Brideshead's flirtatiousness came dangerously close to infidelity on occasion and certainly her long suffering husband had become increasingly concerned about it and distracted in his work. It was worse still when she babbled out those business matters in such company with complete lack of discretion. Already her ill considered public revelations concerning them had caused both Roger and himself considerable embarrassment on several occasions and Lord Castlebridge had taken Roger to task for it and admonished him for his wife's indiscretion. Roger had promised to talk severely to his wife about it and assured Lord Castlebridge that there would be no more such occurrences. Well it appeared that his reprimands, such as they were, had had little effect for, at the weekend, Brenda Brideshead had fallen prey to the malevolent mischief of Stanley Basseldon.

Basseldon was one of their main business rivals and, in Lord Castlebridge's considered opinion, a bounder of the first order. He was a good looking blighter however and just the sort of languorously, arrogant young stud to turn the foolish head of Brenda Brideshead. He had targeted her deliberately at the party she had been attending; there was little doubt of that. He had plied her with champagne and flattery and, before anybody knew it, had wheedled the details of a forthcoming business deal out of her. Armed with this information he had undercut their business arrangement and promptly taken the whole deal away from them, to his own sizeable profit and to Lord Castlebridge's business empire's considerable loss. It was the final straw as far as

Lord Castlebridge was concerned. There was no doubt that Brenda Brideshead was the source of the information that had led to the disaster. Indeed an angry Roger himself had reported that his wife had confessed to the disclosure. He was furious with her and she was now confined to the house in disgrace, he told Lord Castlebridge. Well that was all well and good thought His Lordship but this was a very serious matter and he felt that merely restricting her freedom for a few days would do little to curb the foolish young woman or correct the dangerous cancer that now threatened Lord Castlebridge's very livelihood.

Of course, the most obvious solution would be that, given that Roger and his wife had now become such a liability, he should dispense with the young gentleman's services altogether. Lord Castlebridge didn't want to go that far however if some other solution presented itself. The truth was that he liked young Roger; admired him for his hard working ethic, keen intelligence and high abilities. Lord Castlebridge was somewhat of a mentor to the younger man and it grieved him that Roger's promising career was jeopardised by his foolish wife's imprudent foolishness. What was really needed, thought His Lordship, was some way of effectively curbing her idiocy and teaching her firmly, once and for all, the error of her ways and ensuring that there would be no repetition of her ill advised actions.

Lord Castlebridge paused in his ruminations to listen to the sounds coming across the courtyard. His wife's screams had reached a feverish and manic level by now. Evidently Greenwood was applying himself diligently to his duty and laying the cane down with all the authority His Lordship had commanded. She wouldn't be gambling again in a hurry! He wished that Brenda Brideshead could be so easily corrected of her waywardness. That's what she needed thought Lord Castlebridge; a dose of what his wife was experiencing at this moment! She certainly more than deserved it. If she was his charge then she'd be getting the soundest hiding of her pampered life right now! Regrettably she wasn't his charge and it was unlikely that Roger would discipline her as she deserved.

But if she wasn't his charge, then Roger certainly was and Lord Castlebridge had every right to impose his authority on his junior, even to the extent of insisting that he take immediate and drastic steps to deal with his wife. But how could Lord Castlebridge enforce such an order? What went on in the Brideshead home was surely out of his jurisdiction. He would never be certain that his orders had been carried out. Unless of course he was to supervise Roger's discipline of his wife and witness it to ensure that it was carried out satisfactorily. This was a new thought; the germ of an idea that insinuated itself into his brain and sat there nagging at him. It was not yet a plan but, under the inspiration of his own wife's caning, a seed had been sown.

The last frenzied screams had died away by now and only Lady Castlebridge's soft sobbing could be heard faintly across the courtyard. Greenwood would, by now, be assisting her weeping limp figure from the caning stool. She then had, as was the custom in the house, half an hour to spend kneeling on a stool in the corner, with her skirts hitched up and her hands on her head, in disgrace, before she was finally dismissed from the punishment chamber. Lord Castlebridge glanced at his watch once more. She would then have to exert herself, he noted, for she'd have a little over an hour to repair her appearance and dress for dinner. To give her her due, Lady Castlebridge was invariably well turned out for appearance at the dining table, whatever the circumstances, and His Lordship had every confidence that even the matter of a severe caning would not deviate her from that strict policy.

Lord Castlebridge drained the last of his whisky. He decided to take a quick round of the house. Normally he trusted his senior staff to perform this chore but every once in a while he liked to stamp his authority and run a quick inspection himself. It seemed an admirable notion, at the moment, to ensure himself that there were no other problems he should be concerning himself about. After that of course he'd need to find his valet and begin his own preparations to dress for dinner. Dinner was always a formal affair at Castlebridge Hall and one had appearances to keep up.

CHAPTER 6

Lady Castlebridge gave her husband no cause for dissatisfaction with her appearance at dinner. Her eyes were still somewhat red and swollen from tears it is true and she walked stiffly and gingerly as a result of the throbbing ache in her nether regions. Nevertheless she was becomingly dressed, her make-up reapplied, in place of the ruined mess that had been left in the wake of her caning, and her hair, which had become a tangled ruin as she threw her head from side to side in agony on the caning stool, had been coiffed back into order. She was accompanied by her two personal maids who had helped her dress and they assisted her to her seat at the dining table. One of them carried a soft cushion to place on Her Ladyship's chair and Lady Castlebridge lowered herself carefully onto this, betraying her swollen and tender rear with just a hint of a wince.

Lord Castlebridge's humour had improved little however in the interim and, some of the discoveries he had made during his brief tour of inspection, had not improved it. "Did I tell you that you could sit down Cynthia?" he barked at his wife.

Lady Castlebridge rose hastily to her feet. "No Rupert. I'm sorry Rupert." she bleated fearfully.

He wagged a finger sternly. "I explicitly said that I wished to inspect your bottom at dinner madam! You should have immediately presented yourself for that inspection before seating yourself."

"I'm sorry Rupert." his wife repeated.

"Well come around here then and show yourself

to me."

Lady Castlebridge complied with the order, coming around to her husband's end of the dining table, lifting her dress and lowering her knickers for her husband's examination. Her husband appraised the results with approval. Her Ladyship's swollen buttocks and thighs were admirably marked with livid stripes from the cane and turning purple with bruising. Greenwood, now standing against the wall in attendance and waiting to supervise the serving of the evening meal, had certainly not stinted in his application of the cane to Her Ladyship's rear quarters. It was a thoroughly well caned Lady Castlebridge stood there, with her lip quivering, in humiliation at her husband's inspection. His Lordship nodded at his butler. "Capital Greenwood! A job well done!"

"Thank you My Lord. I always endeavour to give complete satisfaction."

Lord Castlebridge grunted in acknowledgement. "Well Cynthia," he addressed his wife. "I hope you've learned your lesson."

"Yes Rupert." His wife intoned in a low mumble.

"And no more races for you for the foreseeable future understand?"

"Yes Rupert."

"Good girl! Now pull your knickers up, adjust your dress and resume your seat." A slight titter caught Lord Castlebridge's attention. His wife's two personal maids were stood in the background trying to hide their smirks. He frowned. The two girls were another problem he ought to think about. His wife doted on them and was apt to pamper them. The result was that they were spoiled and overly familiar. He'd have to give some thought to an appropriate means of correcting their ways. Still that one could wait for the moment. "You two girls are dismissed!" he barked at them.

"Yes My Lord." They intoned in unison, "Thank you My Lord." The girls curtsied hurriedly and left.

Greenwood cleared his throat. "Shall I instruct the serving girls to serve the soup now My Lord?"

"Before you do there's one more thing Greenwood."

"Yes My Lord?"

"Yes. This evening, before dinner, I had occasion to make a tour of inspection around the house. I am not pleased Greenwood. I am not pleased at all!"

"Indeed My Lord? I am sorry to hear that. In what way were you dissatisfied with your inspection?"

Lord Castlebridge tapped off the points on his fingers. "For one thing the brass and silver work in the long gallery was in an appalling state! It doesn't look as if it's seen a drop of polish in months! Secondly the panelling in the main hall is a disgrace. God only knows what any visitors will think. And thirdly when was the last time the carpets in the guest lounges were hoovered might I ask?"

Greenwood looked deeply concerned, or as concerned as any butler might for whom the lift of a single eyebrow constituted a major expression of astonishment. "I am shocked My Lord."

"Yes and that's not all! I happen to glance out of a window and spied that young Charlotte Grayson girl loafing about behind the East wing when she was supposed to be about her duties."

Greenwood nodded knowingly. "Ah yes! Young Miss Grayson. I've been keeping an eye on her for some time My Lord. I'm afraid idleness is a great fault of hers. I shall take immediate steps to rectify the young lady's indolent ways."

"Good and see to those other matters as well. Standards are slipping Greenwood and I won't have it!"

Greenwood sighed. "I'm afraid I'm inclined to agree with you My Lord. It has come to my attention of late that there has been some considerable lapsing in the standards of work from the household maids. I was discussing this matter with the head housekeeper only this morning."

"Well make sure that some action is taken about it Greenwood."

"You have my word My Lord. I shall consult with Mrs Moorhouse immediately after dinner and attempt to ascertain the culprits involved. Once found I shall see to it personally that they are severely punished and in such a way as to set an example to the rest of the young ladies in the housekeeping department."

"Good! See that you do."

"You may count on me My Lord."

"Excellent. You may serve the soup now Greenwood."

After dinner and a glass of brandy and a cigar in the privacy of his study Lord Castlebridge took his customary evening stroll about the grounds. It was as he was returning from this stroll that he saw the evidence that Greenwood had taken his expression of dissatisfaction and demands for immediate remedial action to heart. Whilst stood by the kitchen gardens at the back of the house he saw four young chambermaids returning to the house from the direction of the copse by the lake. He recognised young Charlotte Carlson immediately and then there was the blond girl, Alicia, the cheeky red headed Betty and that little dark haired Portuguese lass whose name he could never for the life of him recall. The faces of this solemn little procession were a study in fearful misery and the reason for this collective gloom was all too evident. Each girl was carrying a small bundle of freshly cut green twigs four to five feet in length; about seven of eight of them each.

Lord Castlebridge was rather taken aback. It seemed the girls were destined for the birch! He was surprised. He had expected Greenwood to take swift decisive action of course but not something of this severity. A birching was not a light ordeal and usually reserved for serious offences or persistent maladroitness. His Lordship had thought that a few strokes of the cane would have been sufficient. It was plain to see that the increasing laxity of standards around the house had been a matter of serious concern to the senior staff for some time now and his expression of disapproval at dinner had been the final cog to set the wheels in motion and to arrest the erosion of standards around the house by making an example of these four young ladies.

Well it would be a lesson they would not forget in a hurry Lord Castlebridge thought grimly.

Birchings at Castlebridge Hall were always very formalised rituals; severe punishments carried out in front of witnesses. The miscreant was always obliged to go down to the woods to cut the thin twigs themselves and present them at their punishment. If they were not up to the standard required they would be sent back to collect more and additional lashes added to their punishment. Once approved the penitent was then provided with a roll of strong industrial adhesive tape and would bind the twigs together tightly at one end to form a handle and then fashion another binding half way up leaving the last two feet or so as a compact bundle of striking ends. Such a birch switch, wielded with force, scored the skin agonisingly and could even draw blood if the birching was prolonged.

Once the miscreant had fashioned their birch switch it was formally presented to Greenwood who would be responsible for administering the punishment. They would then be obliged to undress completely in front of an audience of their peers and, once naked, be tied firmly, kneeling on a wooden platform at the birching post. They would then be thrashed soundly with the switch they had made with their own hands across the buttocks and thighs. It would be a frightful ordeal. Fifty strokes was the minimum sentence for a birching and, in serious cases, could stretch up to a hundred.

Well it was harsh, thought Lord Castlebridge soberly, but liable to be extremely effective. The four girls would be in no hurry to repeat the experience and the other girls would have no wish to share the same fate once they had witnessed the screaming throes of agony of their colleagues under the birch. Lord Castlebridge expected to see a marked improvement in industriousness from the chambermaids over the coming weeks.

Satisfied that his butler had taken matters firmly in hand, Lord Castlebridge re-entered the Hall and made his way to his study for a nightcap before retiring to bed. It was muggy in his study and he loosened his neck-tie. Damned heat! The windows in Greenwood's pantry, standing in for the library, were open as well and, for the second time that day, the inner courtyard reverberated to the sound of shrill female screams as Greenwood applied the birch. Lord Castlebridge could nearly count every stroke as it landed and he kept a tally in his head as the wailing shrieks echoed in the still evening air. It seemed each girl was administered fifty lashes apart from the last girl to take to the birching post, who, if His Lordship had kept the tally correctly, received seventy five. That would be Charlotte Carlson His Lordship thought correctly. Well she wouldn't be sitting around idling her time after this little lesson in a hurry. She wouldn't be sitting comfortably anywhere for the next few days!

Lord Castlebridge lingered long over his nightcap; long in fact after the last of the shrieks emanating from the library had faded away. While the four weeping girls, who had been so publicly made an example of, knelt in shame on benches against the walls in penance and Greenwood and Mrs Moorhouse had delivered stern warning lectures to their sober faced colleagues, Lord

Castlebridge pondered his own options. A germ of a plan was beginning to form in his mind. Finally he rose from his armchair with a sigh and made his way to his wife's bed-chambers.

CHAPTER 7

Lady Castlebridge was surprised, to say the least, to see her husband. He was a very rare visitor to her private chambers these day. He seldom exercised his conjugal rights any more and she could barely remember the last time he had actually slept in her bed. He preferred, when in residence at the Hall, to sleep in his own chambers adjoining his study and, away from the Hall, had other women to warm his bedclothes. In fact, apart from the formal obligations of social appearance, Lord Castlebridge and his wife led essentially separate lives at the Hall. Lady Castlebridge did not regret this state of affairs. Indeed it suited her rather well for the most part although she was not above exploiting her husband's unfaithfulness to her advantage on occasion. It was not as if she missed her husband's intimate attentions in any way for, with her two delectable maids, she had plenty to divert her in that respect. She would, of course, accommodate her husband on the rare occasions that he required her services in the marital bedchamber but she was generally indifferent to it.

For his part, Lord Castlebridge had curiously complex reasons for attending upon his wife that evening. He was, he was aware, a serial adulterer; the fetching Emilie Dixon at his city office being only one of the assorted paramours he kept squirrelled away. Lord Castlebridge had the decency to feel guilty about his infidelities and corresponding neglect of his beautiful wife. For all his bombastic, authoritarian, male chauvinism, there was a stubborn streak of morality in Lord Castlebridge's inner soul that refused to bow down to his archaic misogyny and imperious autocracy. It was this niggling morality that led to Lord Castlebridge's feelings of guilt and his, entirely delusional, belief that he was doing his wife a disservice by so neglecting her in favour of his mistresses, in flat contradiction of the fact that his wife could have barely cared less about it.

He had even more reason to feel guilty for the moment. He had promised to take Emilie to Geneva for the conference next week and he thought to take her up to the chalet in Zermatt, following the conference, for a day or two of uninhibited domesticity. It was damn likely that his wife would soon be appraised of his plans. He had learned long ago not to underestimate the intelligence gathering capabilities of Cynthia's widespread net of friends and informants and it was probable that his misdeeds in Zermatt would come back to haunt him, especially since he had just had her severely caned.

Although, in his blinkered view, he had been entirely justified in having his wife punished, and that she had certainly deserved it, the honest part of him was bound to admit that the seven thousand pounds his wife had squandered was but a drop in the ocean when compared to the funds he lavished on his various mistresses. Just taking Emilie to Switzerland for a few days would cost far in excess of that amount, even before taking into account the new clothes she would require for her public appearances in Geneva or the inevitable gifts he would be obliged to shower upon her to ensure the quality of her performance in Zermatt.

At the Christmas ball at Smedworth last year, Emilie had openly flaunted the diamond pendant necklace he'd bought her in Antwerp and which had cost him a cool sixteen thousand pounds. His wife had been fully cognisant of the source of the necklace and had made a point of acidly complimenting Emilie on it in his presence. He had cringed inwardly as a result.

So yes, there was a tiny inner kernel within Lord Castlebridge, that acknowledged a degree of hypocrisy in having his wife caned even while his unyielding doctrine demanded it. She had, he was bound to concede, accepted her punishment without protest, and in suitable humility, and he rather admired her for having done so. Nevertheless, having had her punished, he felt duty bound to offer an olive branch of rapprochement. Attending upon her in her chambers was, in his perversely misguided way, his conciliatory gesture to tell her that all was forgiven and he was myopically deluded enough to genuinely believe that she would be grateful for it.

Lord Castlebridge was naturally aware that his wife's own extra-marital conduct was hardly blemishless. He had no illusions that his wife's maids confined their personal services to merely attending to their mistress's wardrobe, cosmetics and coiffure. Oddly enough he was not too concerned about it. He even, and it is a measure of his self delusion, believed it to be partly his own fault. In this ridiculously masculine misapprehension he thought it perfectly understandable that his wife, being so deprived of the more desirable attentions of her husband, would be forced to seek such compensation, as she might, in dalliance with her maids. The horrifying concept that his wife might actually *prefer* the intimate company of her maids had not even begun to impinge itself into his male centred consciousness. For this reason he tended to turn a blind eye to his wife's dalliances with them. They were, after all, he considered, merely a pair of trivial playthings. Of course, had his wife sought solace from his neglect with another man, it would have been entirely a different matter and he would have been furious!

His wife was sat on a pile of cushions at her dressing table, dressed in a silk camisole and matching French knickers, as he entered her chambers; the livid marks on her upper thighs still to be seen below the hem of her knickers. She was being attended to by her two maids, For once the two girls had lost their customary flightiness and looked sober and subdued, as well they might, having just had to console their mistress following her caning. Lady Castlebridge looked up in astonishment as her husband entered. "Why Rupert. This is a surprise!"

Lord Castlebridge dismissed the two maids gruffly before turning to his wife. "I just popped along to see if you are all right Cynthia. Still sore I take it?"

Lady Castlebridge lowered her eyes demurely. "A little Rupert. Thank you for your concern."

"Well I'm sorry that I had to have you caned old thing but you did deserve it you know. I can hardly be expected to maintain discipline in this house if the servants perceive that one rule applies to them and an entirely different one applies to my own wife."

"I quite understand Rupert."

"Well you've been taught your lesson Cynthia so we'll let that be an end to the matter."

His wife, recognising that, in his own awkward way, was offering a peace between them, rose from her stool at the dressing table and took a deep breath. "I... I'm sorry for my foolish behaviour Rupert. You were quite right to have me punished. It won't happen again I assure you."

His Lordship nodded. "You are forgiven Cynthia. Just see that it doesn't happen again mind."

"It won't Rupert I promise you."

"Good! Well I hope that you are not suffering too badly?"

"I'm still a little sore Rupert. Thomas was very severe with me as you asked him to be."

"Better a few days of discomfort Cynthia than ruin and social ostracism with a gambling habit!"

"Yes Rupert."

"Did you get your girls to put some ointment on your bottom?"

"Yes Rupert."

"I've been meaning to talk to you about those two little madams Cynthia. You spoil them far too much."

Lady Castlebridge looked worried. "They're very good to me Rupert."

"Well that's as maybe but I worry that they're getting far too familiar Cynthia and sometimes I'd like to know what they do to earn their keep around here, apart from just fussing around you when you need to prepare yourself. I'm sure your personal grooming doesn't tax too much too much of their time. A bit of good honest work wouldn't harm the pair of them."

"Yes Rupert. I assure you however that the girls know their place and I keep them well in order."

"Perhaps you ought to have them thrashed more regularly."

"I discipline the girls as and when they require it Rupert. However, if it puts your mind at ease, I shall take a strap to them in the morning. Did you just come to enquire after my well being and discuss the running of my boudoir Rupert or was there something else you wished to confer with me about?" Lady Castlebridge was eager to change the subject away from her adored maids.

Lord Castlebridge cleared his throat. "Well Cynthia old thing, it's as hot as the hinges of Hades in my chambers and I'm damned if I can sleep properly. I thought perhaps that I could sleep here tonight."

Lady Castlebridge smiled in understanding and allowed her voice to lower seductively. "Well Rupert! This is a pleasant surprise. It's been a long time since you favoured me by spending a night in my chambers."

Lord Castlebridge shuffled uneasily. "Well you know I've been very busy Cynthia and I often work well into the night and...." he trailed off unable to find any credible excuses.

Lady Castlebridge smiled knowingly and came

forward to place her hands on his shoulders. "I quite understand Rupert. Your er... *business affairs* must keep you so very busy."

Lord Castlebridge swallowed guiltily but the close proximity of his scantily dressed wife, with the scent of her perfume in his nostrils, enticed his interest. He glanced over her shoulder at the reflection of her back in the mirror on her dressing table. As she stood on her tiptoes to clasp his shoulders, her French knickers had ridden up somewhat to reveal just a glimpse of her buttocks, bearing the marks of Greenwood's cane. He found the sight unbearably erotic and felt a quickening in his groin.

Immediately aware of her husband's arousal, Lady Castlebridge saw no reason not to offer an olive branch of her own. She pressed up close to him and murmured. "Well Rupert, if you're staying the night, then you'd best get ready for bed. I could call your valet if you wish or," she plucked gently at the buttons on his jacket, "if you prefer I could help you undress instead."

His Lordship gulped and nodded in assent. "Yes.... er carry on Cynthia."

Her Ladyship had learned a thing or two over the years in mollifying her husband. She gave a low chuckle and knelt on the rug before him and unfastened his trousers. Seeing his wife kneeling in servility before him and easing his trousers down was the tonic Lord Castlebridge's ill humour needed. The front of his under-shorts bulged alarmingly with his suddenly quickened interest. Lady Castlebridge looked at it in amused interest.

"Dear me Rupert? What is this? Surely you are not suddenly rediscovering an interest in your poor old wife? I would have thought you were far too busy with your little playthings at the office to look twice at a withered old thing like me!"

Lord Castlebridge snorted. "Nonsense old girl! You're still a fine looking filly!"

Lady Castlebridge stroked a finger down the bulge in her husband's under shorts. "Why thank you Rupert! I thought you had put me out to grass."

His Lordship was beginning to breath heavily under the ministrations of his wife's caresses. "Not a bit of it!" he protested. He looked down at his wife, kneeling at his feet, her face inches away from the front of his shorts. "I say Cynthia... would you mind....?"

"Oh! Would you like me to....?"

"If you would be so kind. I would consider it a service."

Lady Castlebridge chuckled warmly and eased his under shorts down, liberating his erection. She took his penis in her fingertips almost delicately, as if she were picking up a piece of fine china. Slowly she leaned forward to take it into her mouth. Lord Castlebridge surrendered himself to his wife's skilful dispensations with pleasure yet his mind, having at the moment little else to do, wandered back to the troublesome question of Roger's foolish wife. His eye caught once more a glimpse of his own wife's swollen, streaked posterior. It was in that instance that the plan that had been nagging at him all evening came to clarity in his mind. It was the kind of plan he liked; direct, decisive and one which would deal with the problem for once and for all. It was a plan that would lead directly to the worst day in Brenda Brideshead's pampered life.

CHAPTER 8

With some sort of plan in mind Lord Castlebridge rose the next morning in a considerably better humour. He was humming tunelessly, as he donned the clothes his valet had laid out for him, and feeling in fine spirits. His wife sat up blearily in bad and peered at him. "Are you going in to the office this morning Rupert?"

"Yes there are a few things that need my personal attention Cynthia. I shan't be back for lunch. I'll probably dine at my club. Do you have any plans today Cynthia?"

"Nothing in particular Rupert. I do have to go into Market Castlebridge at some point this afternoon but otherwise nothing much."

"Well will you do me the service of making certain the guest dining room is up to standards Cynthia and inform the kitchen that we'll be expecting guests for dinner on Friday evening?"

Lady Castlebridge opened her eyes in interest. "Oh Really Rupert?"

"Yes Cynthia. I have a mind to invite Roger and his wife over to dinner."

"Oh that'll be nice Rupert. I haven't seen Brenda in simply ages. I shall enjoy that."

Lord Castlebridge grunted and nodded to himself grimly. If the plans solidifying in his mind came to fruition then his wife was anticipating a far more agreeable evening than the one Brenda Brideshead was destined to experience. Before he could reply however there was a knock on the bed chamber door. "Yes! Come in!" he barked.

The door opened to reveal Her Ladyship's two personal maids pushing a small trolley. Lord Castlebridge noted boiled eggs, toast, marmalade, coffee and some deathly glossy, socialite magazine on the trolley. His wife habitually broke her fast in her chambers whereas he preferred to do so in the downstairs dining room over the morning Financial Times. He glanced sharply at the two girls as they curtsied politely. They seemed nervous and unwilling to meet his eye; setting about laying out their mistress's breakfast with hurried efficiency and with little of their habitual frivolity and gaiety. There was evidently a chill wind of reform blowing around the Hall this morning in the wake of Greenwood's disciplinary zeal yesterday.

On his way downstairs to his own breakfast, His Lordship saw further evidence of this new sobriety and diligence. The house keeping maids were up and about early and already industrially about their duties. He nodded with approval. Greenwood's drastic but decisive measures seemed to be bearing early fruit. Perhaps they ought to make it a policy to have a couple of the girls birched every two or three months or so just to keep everybody on their toes!

Passing along the Long Gallery, a solitary figure, on her knees dusting behind a eighteenth century walnut chest, caught his eye. He permitted himself a grim smile. "Ah Young Miss Grayson I see!" he remarked in satisfaction.

Caught by surprise the girl leapt to her feet to curtsy. She winced as she did so. Her rear portions were still paining her this morning. "Good morning My Lord." she intoned tremulously. She was not best pleased at being singled out by the master of the house. She had more a firm policy of keeping as low a profile as possible for the moment.

Lord Castlebridge nodded at her. "Good morning to you too Miss! I'm pleased to see that you're keeping yourself busy! Last night's session with the birch has clearly had a salutary effect on your work ethic!"

Charlotte blushed but curtsied again. "Yes My Lord."

"Still sore this morning?"

"A little My Lord."

"Well turn around and drop your knickers and let me have a look!"

Charlotte blushed crimson and swallowed but she did as she was bid, turning around to hoist up her skirt and petticoat and lowering her knickers to expose her bottom. Lord Castlebridge leaned forward to examine the result with interest. It was little wonder she was walking stiffly this morning or that her knickers were chafing at her bottom as she curtsied. The contusions of the previous evening were still clearly to be seen and her bottom was still puffily swollen and extensively bruised. Still, reassuringly, there seemed to be no scarring. She'd be carrying the marks around for a few days yet but she should heal up satisfactorily. He grunted in satisfaction. "Well no permanent damage there young lady. You'll be sore for a few days but that's no bad thing. It'll serve to remind to pay more attention to your duties."

"Yes sir." mumbled the deeply humiliated young lady.

"Well pull your knickers up and be about your business then girl and lets have no more of your slacking off in future."

Charlotte readjusted her dress and curtsied once more. "Yes My Lord. Thank you My Lord. I'll do my best My Lord."

Lord Castlebridge regarded her not unkindly. "Well see that you do young lady. Now you've had one good lesson so see to it that you don't have to suffer another. You'll find me as ready to reward as to punish young lady so apply yourself to your duties well and you'll go far."

"Yes My Lord, thank you My Lord."

"Very well! Carry on!"

Charlotte curtsied and returned to her work as Lord Castlebridge resumed his way to the dining room in fine humour. He breakfasted heartily on poached eggs and kippers and not even the latest portents of doom from the financial pages of the morning newspapers could dampen his spirits now that he had formulated a good workable solution to the problem of Roger Brideshead's foolish wife.

"Will you be going into the city today My Lord?" asked Greenwood as he replenished His Lordship's coffee.

"Yes Greenwood. I'll need a car in about fifteen minutes."

"Very good My Lord. I shall inform the chauffeur."

"Ah yes Greenwood and a capital job last night; capital!"

"Thank you My Lord. I endeavour to provide satisfaction."

"I bumped into young Charlotte Grayson in the Long Gallery looking as if she won't sit down for a week!"

"Yes My Lord. I felt it incumbent on me to be particularly stern with young Miss Carlton given her recent record My Lord."

"Quite right! Quite right Greenwood! Couldn't agree more. You seem to have acted with exemplary firmness Greenwood."

"I felt it justified My Lord in view of the relaxation of standards that have become evident in recent weeks and which you so rightly pointed out at dinner yesterday evening. It may be that you feel I have been somewhat harsh however."

"Not a bit of it Greenwood. You have my full backing in this. In fact it crossed my mind, whilst I was talking to Charlotte Grayson, that it may not be a bad idea to instigate more regular punishments of this order to make sure that standards are maintained in future."

"Yes My Lord. A similar thought occurred to me. Certainly it would be no bad thing to have a firmer hand on the tiller in these troubled times. This younger generation seems to sadly lack the discipline we were accustomed to in former times My Lord."

"Quite so Greenwood." Lord Castlebridge looked at his watch. "Well we'll have to talk more of this at our leisure Greenwood. Right now I have to grab some papers from my study. Make sure my car is ready Greenwood."

"I shall attend to it immediately My Lord."

CHAPTER 9

It was a little before ten in the morning when Lord Castlebridge's Rolls Royce drew up outside his city offices. Making his way inside, His Lordship was greeted at his desk by his private secretary; a young lady whose efficiency and devoted loyalty made her indispensable to the smooth running of his city affairs. She was also, in her smart white blouse, knee length pale grey skirt over long slender legs clad in dark stockings and her long dark hair, an extremely ornamental addition to the mundane world of the office. The perfume she wore might have been called "Desert Mist", or some such nonsense, but it would more properly be described as "justifiable grounds for molestation" Lord Castlebridge considered, as always be-glamoured by the sultry allure of the young lady who kept his city office running with such admirable precision.

"Good Morning Sir." she greeted him with a curtsy, her voice a siren's call of invitation.

"Morning Emilie." His Lordship intoned as he took his seat behind his desk.

"The review papers for the Carter Branniston contract are in your in-tray Sir and I've taken the liberty of laying out the share holders' report of the Allied Textiles Conglomerate on your desk for your perusal Sir."

"Excellent Emilie. And the conference next week in Geneva?"

"Tickets are confirmed in business class for the afternoon Swissair flight on the Monday Sir as you requested."

"Capital! And the accommodation Emilie?"

Emilie lowered her voice silkily. "We have adjoining suites in Le Richemond Sir as you wished."

"Splendid! Is Mr Brideshead in the building?"

"No Sir. He is in conference with the solicitors regarding the Carter Branniston contract. He expects to be back in the office around eleven Sir."

"Ah of course. Well will you tell him to see me in my office as soon as he comes in?"

"Of course Sir. Is there anything else I can do for you?"

"No I think that will be all Emilie."

Emilie leaned forward over the desk invitingly. "Are you sure there's nothing else you require Sir?"

Lord Castlebridge frowned at her. "Now Emilie! Business hours remember!"

She pouted at him. "But it's been three whole weeks!"

"Behave Emilie or do you want me to take the strap to you?"

She tossed her hair back in a sulk. "I should be so lucky! I can't remember the last time you spanked me!"

Lord Castlebridge looked at his beautiful secretary in surprise. "Are you implying that you actually *want* me to beat you Emilie?"

"Hmph! It would be better than no attention at all!"

"I hardly think that you can have any cause for complaint on that score Emilie. God knows you cost me enough money! New car, luxury flat on the waterfront, the Lord alone knows how much in clothes and jewellery! Hardly evidence of neglect I would have thought!"

"You caned your wife yesterday didn't you?" asked Emilie with a bewildering change of tack.

Lord Castlebridge sighed. So this was what this was all about! He didn't want to know how Emilie could have learned that so quickly. Her network of spies was pervasive and infallible and he had suspected for some time that she had her informants within the walls of Castlebridge Hall. "I did not cane my wife Emilie. I had my butler do it for me."

"Hmmph!" Emilie repeated. "And was it your butler who spent the night in your wife's chambers as well? Perhaps I should ask him to attend to my needs as well since you so seldom appear to have the time."

His Lordship stifled a groan. "Now, now Emilie. I've been very busy as you know. As for sleeping with my wife I do have to keep up appearances as you well know. Now stop sulking and, if you're a good girl, I'll buy you something nice in Geneva and I'll see if we can't manage a couple of days in the chalet up at Zermatt after the conference."

Her eyes sparkled in sudden delight. "Really Rupert? That would be lovely!"

"We'll see Emilie. No promises now. It depends on your behaviour. Now away with you and be about your business and don't forget I want to see Roger as soon as he comes in."

She swept out of the room happily and Lord Castlebridge leaned over his desk and shook his head despairingly. It was ironic he thought. He had

had his wife caned yesterday for squandering the trifling sum of seven thousand pounds yet that was but a tithe of the outlay it cost him to keep his captivating mistress happy! If his wife ever had the occasion to peruse his "expenses" account she'd fall in a dead faint!

Still that was by the by. It was almost expected of a man in his position to keep a mistress or two and he would never rub his wife's face in it through indiscretion or do anything foolish such as run away with the girl. He would give his wife all that she would ever need. Emilie and her ilk was his hobby, albeit a damned expensive one.

For the next hour His Lordship busied himself at his in-tray and sundry items of business demanding his attention. There was nothing particularly difficult to contend with however and he had tied up most of the loose ends before, a little after eleven o'clock, Emilie emerged once more to announce that Roger Brideshead was waiting without in response to His Lordship's summons.

"Ah splendid! Bung him in then Emilie."

"Yes Sir!" Emilie acknowledged, with what Lord Castlebridge considered an unnecessary emphasis on the word "Sir", and turned towards the door to comply with a deliberately provocative wriggle to her hips. His Lordship gave an exasperated sigh and made a mental note to himself to pack a couple of lengths of good stout rattan cane in his cases for Geneva next month. A moment or two later the door opened to admit the nervous looking figure of Roger Brideshead.

"Ah there you are Roger." Lord Castlebridge

turned to his secretary, still at the door. “Could you rustle up coffee for two Emilie? Sit down Roger. Take a seat.”

Roger obeyed, to a certain degree reassured that at least he wasn’t going to be kept kicking his heels on the carpet which he had considered an all too likely scenario given the cloud currently over him as a result of his wife’s criminal indiscretion. He had been dreading this face to face meeting with Lord Castlebridge and was honest enough with himself to realise that his career hung by a thread. His Lordship had ruthlessly sacked juniors for far less than the disaster which had occurred because of his wife’s garrulous tongue and foolish flirtatiousness.

His wife Brenda was at home. The Brideshead household did not possess a dog but if it had then the dog would have been currently sharing quarters with the disgraced mistress of the house. Roger had delivered the longest, most detailed lecture of their married life to his chagrined wife yesterday evening and, for once, she’d been sufficiently aware of her culpability to think of arguing back. He had cut off her allowance and forbidden her under any circumstances to leave the house without his permission; adding, acidly, that if, after his forthcoming interview with Lord Castlebridge, they still had a house for her to be confined to then it would be a miracle of sorts!

His wife had taken the lecture in subdued and uncharacteristic silence. She was a seriously frightened young woman. The word “divorce” hadn’t actually been mentioned but, given that her philandering with other men had finally caught up with her and threatened ruin on the financial security of her marriage, it was dangling unmentioned above her with all the ominous doom of Damocles' sword. She was conforming to the restrictions place upon her with impeccable obedience but hers was the lonely vigil of the condemned and even the delivery of this month's Cosmopolitan magazine was failing to alleviate her gloom.

Lord Castlebridge wasted no time on preliminaries with Roger. "Well Roger," he began," I think we both know what it is that we need to discuss."

Roger took a deep breath and prepared to deliver the speech he had been assiduously practising in his head. "Yes sir. I can only repeat what I said to you on the phone and offer my most profound apologies sir. You have my most solemn reassurances sir that I'll not allow anything of this nature to occur again. I have..."

Lord Castlebridge raised a hand to cut him off in full flow. "Roger I have had theses assurances before! The last time we were embarrassed by your wife's indiscretion you assured me then that it would never happen again. Yet here we are again and even worse! Have you any idea what the loss of this contract means in financial terms to this business?"

Roger nodded penitently. "Yes sir. I'm aware of the figures."

"Well then you'll be doubtless aware that we can ill afford to lose business in times like these as a result of your wife' inability to keep her mouth shut! I'm annoyed about this business Roger, damned annoyed!"

Roger felt a light sweat break out on his forehead. "Yes sir! You have every right to be annoyed. Again I apologise."

Lord Castlebridge dismissed the apology with a wave of his hand. "Saying sorry is all well and good Roger but that won't help mend the damage here. Losing this client was a serious loss to this business and I'm afraid the responsibility for that loss must be laid entirely at your feet."

Roger swallowed. "Yes sir."

"When somebody joins this business Roger, especially one with such high responsibilities as you, then I am entitled to expect complete discretion from them and to be able to trust them implicitly to divulge none of the inner workings of this business to outside sources. You have manifestly failed in that trust Roger. Because of that you have become a liability to this company."

Roger felt a cold chill blow over him. "Are you going to sack me then sir?"

Lord Castlebridge pondered before replying. "Let's just say that I am weighing my options Roger. I have made no final decision as yet."

Roger felt the faint twitches of hope. He wasn't finished yet. "Sir I can only assure you once again that, should you give me another chance, I will do everything in my power to ensure that nothing like this ever happens again."

"Including giving up your wife Roger?"

Roger blinked in shock. "I...I'm sorry sir?"

"I said giving up your wife Roger! If I asked you to choose between this company and your wife would you do it?"

"I... I don't know sir... I never thought..." Roger was floundering desperately. Finally he took a deep breath and grasped his hands together. "I'm sorry sir. I know Brenda has her faults but well...I wouldn't want...I mean I suppose lots of chaps would consider divorce under the circumstances but...." Roger shook his head miserably "Well I still love her you see sir. I don't want to lose her. I mean if you feel that you need to dispense with my services sir, well I understand but my wife... well I vowed to take her for better or for worse sir. You wouldn't want to see me be so lacking in moral fibre as to forget such a solemn undertaking at the first signs of rocky shoals would you? I know she's far from perfect sir, and God knows she drives me to distraction often enough, but... well I guess I'll stick by the old girl sir even if it means losing my job."

Lord Castlebridge leaned back in his chair in satisfaction. It was the answer he had wanted hear. His opinion of Roger would have been greatly diminished if the young man had been all too willing to sacrifice his wife to save his own skin. He took a long appraising look at his junior. If Roger ever did divorce his wife there'd certainly be no shortage of young fillies eager to take her place for he was a fine looking young man with sandy hair, clear grey eyes and lean handsome build. He was also, the current crisis notwithstanding, a fine asset to the company for he was intelligent, gifted and industrious. Lord Castlebridge certainly didn't want to let him go but, if his scheme to solve this problem was to bear fruition, then his junior had to fear that dismissal was a very real possibility.

There was a pause as Emilie served the coffee. Lord Castlebridge took his time to collect his thoughts. "Well then Roger it seems as if we are at an impasse. Since I can't seemingly trust you to curb your wife's indiscretion and you don't wish to let her go then what am I to do with you?"

Roger shrugged ruefully. "I don't know sir! Kick me out I suppose."

"I would like to avoid that if it were at all possible Roger but it may be that you give me no choice." Lord Castlebridge paused to take a sip of his coffee. "I may be able to save your job yet Roger however."

Roger's hopes soared. "Oh really sir? I promise you that you won't regret it! I..."

Lord Castlebridge held up a warning finger. "I said "may" Roger. I have by no means made a final decision."

Roger nodded eagerly. "Of course sir. I fully understand."

"If I do retain you Roger it will be only on the strict condition that you agree with me to take the sternest measures possible to ensure that there is absolutely no repetition of this of this sort of thing in the future. Would you agree to that?"

"Yes of course sir! Naturally."

"I will determine those measures Roger and I'll expect you to abide by my decision regarding them. Is that also agreeable to you?"

"Yes sir. Absolutely sir."

"Furthermore, Roger your wife will have to abide by my decision too and agree to the measures I decide upon. Will she do that?"

Roger nodded grimly. "Yes sir. I will ensure that she agrees upon whatever you decide sir."

"If that is the case Roger, then I might be able to save your position here. I will expect strict adherence to my wishes however. Otherwise I'm afraid I would not feel any longer justified in trusting you with a position of responsibility within this company. Is that fully understood?"

"I understand completely sir."

"Very well. I shall take a day or two to finalise my decision. I would like you and your wife to come for dinner at the Hall on Friday evening. I shall be able to tell the both of you my decision then. Would that be convenient for you?"

Roger nodded in renewed hope. "Of course sir."

"In that case we'll leave it there until Friday Roger. In the meantime I advise you to talk to your wife and impress upon her that it is imperative that she agrees fully to my decision regarding this matter."

"Yes sir. I will certainly do so."

"Excellent! Now if you'll excuse me Roger I have some affairs to see to."

Roger jumped hastily to his feet. "Of course sir! I shall leave you to it."

Once Roger had left Lord Castlebridge leaned back in his chair in great satisfaction. That had gone rather well he thought. He had been somewhat less than candid with Roger for there was no real pressing business to attend to, now that he had cleared his in-tray. He rather thought a leisurely lunch at his club was in order. He pushed the bell on his desk. Emilie appeared within seconds. "Ah Emilie! Could you call my car please? I shall be dining at the club."

"Yes sir."

Lord Castlebridge paused. "Oh yes and Emilie...."

"Yes sir?"

"I understand you've been batting your eyelashes around that young man in sales... what's his name now... Gordon... that's it... Andrew Gordon!"

Emilie paled "Only in a professional capacity sir!"

"See that it remains so Emilie. If I hear that you've been up to mischief with him I shall be forced to summon you to the Hall," Lord Castlebridge paused for effect. "To be birched Emilie!"

The blood drained from Emilie's face. "You'd birch me?"

Lord Castlebridge grinned wickedly. "Not me Emilie! I will delegate the task to my butler. He did an excellent job with the birch on some of our house maids yesterday evening and I'm sure he can spare a few minutes, amidst his duties, to demonstrate his proficiency on you!"

Emilie swallowed nervously. "I'm sure you'll have no reason to reproach my behaviour sir."

Lord Castlebridge rose and picked up his coat and hat. "Make sure that you adhere to that resolve Emilie or, mark my words, it'll be the birch for you and you can forget about Geneva next week!"

"Yes sir. Of course sir." said Emilie, while trying to think furiously who His Lordship's spy in the office was.

"Excellent. Now my car if you please." Lord Castlebridge sauntered out of the office well content. It was good to crack the whip once in a while! It was Wednesday. There'd be roast lamb, mint sauce and boiled new potatoes at the club today. He was rather looking forward to it.

CHAPTER 10

Lord Castlebridge, his head filled with other concerns, dismissed the matter from his mind for most of the rest of the week. It wasn't until Thursday evening, upon his return to the Hall, that it occurred to him that there might be some hitch in his plans. In some concern therefore he made his way to the library.

To his surprise, Lord Castlebridge found that the library was already occupied. Greenwood, looking uncharacteristically informal in his shirt sleeves, was present and evidently in the middle of some corporeal labour. The other occupant of the room was a young girl that Lord Castlebridge vaguely recognised as one of the latest additions to the domestic staff; having been only been in service at the Hall for a few months. It was, however, difficult to be certain because the young girl was currently strapped down over the caning stool with her hair draped over her tear sodden face in tangled ruin. Her exposed posterior was well laced with vivid scarlet stripes and she was the obvious reason for Greenwood's current labours, even without the further evidence of the long cane in his hand.

Lord Castlebridge halted in the doorway. "Oh I'm sorry Greenwood." he apologised. "I didn't realise you were using the place for the moment."

"That's quite all right My Lord. Were you requiring the chamber for any purpose?"

"Not particularly Greenwood. I didn't wish to disturb you."

"Not at all My Lord. I was merely engaged in

caning young Miss Renford here. However if you require the use of the chamber I could always adjourn proceedings and complete her chastisement a little later."

"No, no Greenwood. I wouldn't hear of it! I don't wish to interrupt you in the execution of such an important duty. I only popped along for a minute to assure myself that the library was back up and running again."

"I see sir. Well, as you can see, the workmen completed the repairs yesterday. I had the furniture moved back in and the caning stool reinstalled this morning My Lord. It is, I confess, still a little dusty and in need of a good cleaning. However, Mrs Moorhouse assures me that she has allocated a contingent of maids to the task of cleaning the place thoroughly in the morning."

"Capital! That is most satisfactory Greenwood. I may be requiring the use of it tomorrow evening after dinner. We have guests coming who I want to show the library to and I was rather afraid that it would still be a bit of a mess."

"You may be assured that the chamber will be spotless My Lord. I shall impress upon the young ladies responsible for the cleaning that there is to be no stint in their efforts, inform them that I shall personally inspect the chamber afterwards and cane the lot of them should it fail to meet a satisfactory standard My Lord."

"Excellent Greenwood. You put my mind at ease." Lord Castlebridge walked forward the better to see the young girl still snivelling miserably in her prone position over the caning stool. "So! Young

Rebecca Renford is it? I thought I recognised her. Not been with us long has she?"

"No My Lord. Miss Renford joined us shortly before Christmas."

"Well she hasn't wasted time finding her way to the library! Is this her first caning then?"

"Her first *formal* caning My Lord." Greenwood amended. "I have, on a previous occasion, had reason to cane her more informally and Mrs Moorhouse tells me that she has had to take the strap to her on a number of occasions, but this is the first time she has been required to report to the library for a formal punishment on the caning stool."

"I see and just what has she done to earn herself this honour!"

"Nothing specific My Lord. However, her poor record became apparent at her review this morning and it was felt that a salutary caning was merited."

Lord Castlebridge raised an eyebrow inquiringly. "Review? What on earth's this all about?"

Greenwood bit his lip uncertainly. "Ah yes My Lord. I have been meaning talk to you about this at your convenience sir. It is a policy I have instigated on my own initiative following our conversation concerning the falling standards in the Hall earlier this week. I hope I have not exceeded my authority by already implementing the policy without consulting you."

"Just what is this policy Greenwood?"

"Well sir you expressed concern that the standards of work were below expectations of late and, as you are aware, I had several of the worst transgressors birched earlier in the week. That however seemed to be merely a temporary stop gap measure to address a current situation. As far as it goes, the action would appear to have been successful and, for the moment at least, has sufficed to reverse the haphazard attitude to work ethic and personal conduct that has been apparent over the past few weeks. That was all well and good, as far as it went, but I feared that, once the memory of the birching had faded, the young ladies of the Hall would slip all too easily back into complacency and neglect. I felt, therefore, that a longer term policy was required to maintain the high standards expected and one which would continually serve to remind the young ladies of the consequences of neglecting those standards. With this view in mind, I proposed a new stratagem at the meeting of department heads on Tuesday evening."

Lord Castlebridge nodded in approval. "Well this all sounds very admirable. What exactly did you come up with?"

"Well My Lord, at the meeting, it was decided to implement a policy of regular reviews for every junior servant in the house. We thought to require each young lady to appear before a review panel, of senior staff members, regularly, in a formal setting, to review their work performance and personal conduct over the past months. Those young ladies that have demonstrated exemplary behaviour and appliance to their duties could be then rewarded, as a result of a favourable decision at the formal review, whereas those having displayed a less than satisfactory adherence to the standards required, could expect to be censured and have an appropriate punishment assigned to them. With each young lady aware that she would be facing a formal review in the future, we thought it would provide an admirable incentive to ensure improved behaviour and diligence."

Lord Castlebridge hooked his thumbs into his waste coat pockets and rocked on his heels; a sure sign that he approved of something. "I like the sound of this Greenwood! How often would you formally convene these review panels?"

"We are still discussing these details My Lord but, as an initial premise, we are thinking that those girls with a good record should have their reviews twice a year. However those with a less admirable record should be called before a review board quarterly. However there is room for a good deal of flexibility in the arrangement. Any girl, for example, who failed her review and was censured, would be required to face another review within three months, or whatever period the board decided, irrespective of her record previous to that."

"Very sensible. How would you keep record of the girl in question's behaviour? Would it be verbal testimony from her superiors at the review board?"

Greenwood shook his head. "No My Lord." He laid his cane aside for the moment and gestured to a table set to one side. "If I may be permitted to show you."

Lord Castlebridge allowed himself to be led to the table. There were two items on the table. One of these Greenwood pushed aside distastefully with one finger. They were Rebecca's knickers and they were soaking wet. Whilst awaiting her caning, the unfortunate young girl had been unable to contain herself and had wet her knickers in her terror. With the offensive object out of the way, Greenwood directed Lord Castlebridge's attention to a slim folder.

"This My Lord, is Miss Renford's personal file. Each of the young ladies in the Hall is to be issued with such a file which they will be required to hand in to their superior at the end of each working day. The body of the file consists of a day to day diary with boxes to be ticked by their superior on their performance that day: "very good", "good", "satisfactory", "poor", "very poor" and so forth. There is also a space for their superior to write any observations on the young lady's conduct that day that may be relevant. Letters of commendation can also be inserted into the file and I intend to make it a standard practice, henceforth, that all punishments applied must be recorded in writing, detailing the offence and the punishment awarded for it, and the record placed in each girl's personal file. Hitherto we have only recorded formal disciplinary actions, in the library, in the library's official punishment ledger. As a result of that we have often lost sight of minor infractions and petty misbehaviour that may be indicative of chronic symptoms of ill discipline that are in need of serious correction."

"That seems very wise Greenwood." Lord Castlebridge opened Rebecca's file. "Not a lot in here though."

"No sir. Obviously we have just started to issue these files and they naturally haven't been in existence long enough yet to accumulate a body of evidence. In Miss Renford's case here the board, by necessity, relied upon verbal evidence."

"I see. So you have already begun to convene these review boards then?"

"Yes My Lord. We held the formal reviews of six girls this morning. On my return from my annual vacation, it is my intention to hold reviews for every young girl in the Hall in the space of two weeks."

"Excellent. And what were the findings of the reviews this morning?"

"I shall have a copy of the minutes of the review board forwarded to your study sir but, in short, I will summarise them for you. One young lady was commended for her behaviour and admirable attitude to her work and awarded extra privileges as a result. Two young ladies were deemed satisfactory. There were also two girls who were admonished for less than satisfactory performance, scheduled for an early follow up review and formally warned that they would be caned should their performance not have improved markedly by that time. In the case of Miss Renford however, it was decided that her record was sufficiently poor to merit immediate action, so she was subsequently sentenced to fifty strokes of the cane and ordered to report to the library, immediately after tea, to receive her punishment."

"Well I must say that all this is a capital idea Greenwood. Most meritorious! I am delighted that you have taken such immediate and effective steps to address my concerns and you have my full support in these new policies."

"Thank you My Lord."

"Well deserved Greenwood and, now, I shall not detain you any further in the execution of your duty."

Greenwood picked up his cane once more. "Thank you sir. If you'll forgive me therefore..."

"Of course. How many more has the lass coming to her anyway?"

"Miss Renford had received twenty nine strokes before you arrived in the library My Lord. She has a further twenty one due, to complete the sentence allotted to her at the review board."

"Well I trust you to do your customary excellent job on her Greenwood and teach her a lesson she won't forget in a hurry."

"Thank you sir. I shall endeavour to impress upon the young lady the gravity with which her misconduct is regarded."

"Glad to hear it. Well carry on Greenwood."

"Thank you My Lord."

With that, Lord Castlebridge strode to the door and departed. He paused for a moment in the passage outside to listen however. A loud report of rattan cane on bare flesh, and the accompanying howling scream, announced that Rebecca Renford's temporary respite had ended and that her caning had commenced once more. Lord Castlebridge allowed himself a grim smile of satisfaction and walked away, well content that matters were in hand.

CHAPTER 11

If Lord Castlebridge was content with the progress of events, it was more than could be said for Roger and Brenda Brideshead as they drove through the English countryside in Roger's new BMW on Friday evening. There was a subdued silence in the car and their thoughts were far from the culinary pleasures to be looked forward to at Castlebridge Hall that evening. They had seemingly talked of little else but this coming confrontation since Roger's ominous interview with Lord Castlebridge on Wednesday. "What do you think he's decided to do?" asked Brenda in a low murmur for what felt like the thousandth time.

"I've no idea honey." her husband replied worriedly. "Whatever it is though we have to abide by his decision. We've no choice!"

Brenda nodded soberly. On that point they were in total agreement. Over the past few days they had taken a long appraisal of their lives together and the extent to which their prosperity and security depended upon the continued good will and patronage of Lord Castlebridge. Roger's position within the company was extremely lucrative. It paid for their new house, Roger's BMW, Brenda's Aston Martin, which she loved like a sister, their holidays in the Seychelles, the little cottage in Cornwall, Brenda's all consuming, extensive wardrobe, Roger's membership of his golf club and even Brenda's busy social life. Without Lord Castlebridge's decision to retain him, Roger would just be a disgraced and overly young, unemployed executive in hard economic times. They stood to lose everything.

Brenda was doubly frightened. To a certain degree she had already learned a lesson for she was overwhelmingly aware that the blame for this entire crisis could be laid squarely at her feet. She realised now what folly it had been to let that devilishly handsome young man ply her with drinks and flatter her. How was she to have known he was a representative of a rival company? He had just seemed so appreciative of her and attentive to her. Roger was always so busy with work these days. She'd felt neglected. Roger never seemed to have the time to pay her all those little attentions a woman needed so, when the young man had introduced himself to her at the party, it had made her feel attractive and wanted. She knew she had flirted dangerously with him. Nothing had happened beyond that but she knew she had given her husband more than enough grounds to be seriously angry with her, even without the information she had so carelessly furnished the treacherous young predator.

Roger had reported the exact details of his interview with Lord Castlebridge. The blood had drained from her face when he'd described the moment when His Lordship had asked what Roger would do if forced to choose between his career and his wife. The foundations of her life had trembled beneath her. Her husband losing his job was catastrophe enough. Losing her husband didn't bear thinking about. For all her flirtatious foolishness Brenda adored her husband. She just wished he had more time for her.

CHAPTER 12

In her boudoir at Castlebridge Hall Lady Castlebridge was finishing her own preparations for dinner in front of her dressing table mirror. She was feeling quite pleased with herself. She still had the marks on her bottom from Tuesday's caning of course, although they were fading by now, and her rear still felt a little stiff and gave her occasional twinges. Nevertheless she had good reasons to feel pleased. The little snippets of information she had caused to come to her husband's ear regarding Emilie Dixon and Andrew Gordon in his office were bearing fruit! Rumour had it that he had threatened to have his secretary birched! Her Ladyship glowed at the thought. That was one birching she wanted to be a witness to! She was monitoring events carefully there. That little madam would slip up again sooner or later and Her Ladyship knew just how to bring the fact to her husband's attention.

Lady Castlebridge knew all about Emilie of course; and the little French piece of fluff her husband kept in the company's European office in Paris: AND the little Chinese girl in their Far Eastern bureau! Lady Castlebridge may have been subservient to her husband in the Hall but she wasn't stupid! As has been mentioned, she was rather unconcerned about her husband's harem of mistresses around the globe. Somehow it seemed almost fitting that her husband had his little affairs to keep him occupied. The fact that he had at least three that she knew of was more encouraging than anything. The more the merrier as far as she was concerned! One serious rival might have worried her but her husband trying to juggle three little indulgences all at once hardly indicated any particular single infatuation. She was the one with the wedding ring after all. She was the one with the title. The others were just dalliances her husband would dispense with when he became bored with them.

The other thing about her husband's affairs was that it kept his attention firmly elsewhere for long periods; attention away in other words from Her Ladyship's own extra-marital activities. Her Ladyship had desires and needs of her own and, unlike her husband's, they were relatively inexpensive. She patted a wayward lock of her luxurious blond mane into place and smiled at her reflection in the mirror. "Well girls? Do I pass muster?" she asked.

Suzette leaned over her shoulder and grinned at her in the mirror. "You 'ave looking, 'ow you say it, gorgeous madame!"

Lady Castlebridge chuckled deeply and reached behind to stroke a languid finger down the side of Suzette's face. "Thank you my little flatterer!" she murmured.

Maria leaned across her other shoulder, her long hair tickling the bare flesh exposed by her sleeveless dress. "You're just beautiful ma'am!"

Lady Castlebridge laughed softly in great contentment and wrapped an arm around each of the two young girls, drawing them close to her affectionately. They were exceedingly pretty tonight. For reasons of his own her husband had commanded that her two personal maids attend upon the party at dinner tonight. Lady Castlebridge was vaguely worried about that but she hoped they were there just to be attractive adornments: a pleasant visual diversion for their guests that night. They certainly looked the part. They were dressed in the standard Castlebridge Hall servant's garb of pretty little maid's uniforms; black with lacy white trimmings, white pinafores and the frill of lacy petticoats showing below the hem of their short dresses above long shapely legs.

"Now you two girls behave yourselves at dinner tonight." she warned them. "His Lordship has been in a strange mood all week and we don't want to be making more work for Greenwood by having your pretty little bottoms caned, now do we?"

Maria looked sulkily defiant. "We'd rather he had us caned than you ma'am!" she pouted rebelliously. "We hated him for having you caned on Tuesday!"

"That'll do Maria. Remember he's the one that puts money on the table and he's the master in this house so remember your place. If we all have to put up with the odd caning now and again to assuage his ill humour, then that's just the way it is and we have to accept it." She let her hands slip from the girls' waists, down over their bottoms and let them come to rest on their legs, below the hem of their dresses, where she tickled the backs of their thighs teasingly. "Cheer up girls! Next week he's going away to Geneva for a conference. He's taking his secretary so doubtless there'll be other "business" to attend to. With a bit of luck he'll be away for the whole week."

"Hmmph! So 'e is taking la salope wiz 'im is 'e?" observed Suzette sourly. "Elle est rien en comparaison de vous madame!"

Lady Castlebridge allowed herself a small smile. "Don't worry about her Suzy! That little madam's got her come-uppance due! A little dicky bird tells me that there's a nice stout birch switch with her name on it!"

Maria grinned evilly. "That I want to see!"

Lady Castlebridge chuckled. "Well let's just say that that's a work in progress. In the meantime, while His Lordship's in Switzerland, I thought we might take a little constitutional at the cottage in Devon: just the three of us! What do you say?"

The two girls lit up with happiness. "Oh yes ma'am!" enthused Maria, "That would be lovely!"

"Well we'll see. Now come on girls, give me a kiss and then we'd better go downstairs to receive our guests."

Dinner, it has to be said, was not a great success. There was certainly nothing wrong with the fare on offer to be sure. The sorbet was tangy and icy cold; the consommé clear and enriched with sherry. The entrée of smoked salmon, shallots and capers was unimaginative but perfectly sound and the Chateaubriand of tenderloin steak in Bordelais sauce served with Pommes Coq D'or for the main course was excellent. Nor could there have been any complaints over the crème brulee served as a dessert or the fine selection of cheeses to accompany the port. What was lacking over the dinner table was any sort of agreeable conversation and Castlebridge Hall's head chef would have torn what little remained of his hair from his head and retired to his bed in a decline had he witnessed the sullen silence which greeted every masterpiece of his to grace the table.

Roger barely tasted the food placed before him, so tense was he with foreboding, and fielded Lord Castlebridge's occasional remarks with mumbled monosyllables. Brenda was even more subdued and sat miserably at the table all too aware of the dark cloud of disgrace hanging over her. Lady Castlebridge attempted to engage her in small talk but Lord Castlebridge, other than the formalities of common courtesy, ignored her completely to emphasise the isolation of her shame. Eventually even Lady Castlebridge's conversation dried up as the full impact of Brenda's disgrace began to dawn on her. She could see the undercurrents moving in only one direction. She liked Brenda and at this moment she began to feel truly sorry for her.

Finally Greenwood served the coffee and, for the gentlemen at least, balloons of fine cognac and Roger could take it no longer. "Sir," he began, "Brenda and I once again wish to offer our profound apologies for what has occurred over the business you've so rightly taken me to task for."

Lord Castlebridge raised his eyes to peer ironically over his brandy glass. "Indeed Roger?"

Roger nodded eagerly. "Yes we do sir. Brenda is mortified and ashamed of her indiscretion and wishes to assure you that she will never let anything like it occur again."

Lord Castlebridge raised an eyebrow. “And has your wife no tongue to speak for herself Roger?”

Brenda swallowed and turned pale. “Yes My Lord,” she mumbled miserably. “I...I’m truly sorry. Really I am.”

Lord Castlebridge regarded her slowly. “And do you think that your apologies are sufficient Brenda; sufficient to assure me that there will be no repetition of your foolishness?”

Brenda lowered her eyes and gripped the fabric of her skirt with her hands to still their trembling. “I...I don’t know m...My Lord. I... I just want to say how... how sorry I am.”

“I’m sure Brenda never meant any harm by it Rupert...” Lady Castlebridge interposed hastily.

Lord Castlebridge glared at his wife. “Thank you Cynthia but I had already arrived at that conclusion independently! If I thought, for one moment, that this young lady here had deliberately sabotaged my business arrangements then I would have sacked Roger a week ago and neither he nor his wife would be dining at my table!”

His Lordship’s words were a whip crack in the tension of the room. Lady Castlebridge retreated into glum silence as her husband returned to address Brenda. “Whatever foolish notion crossed your mind to babble out the details of an important transaction to one of our most bitter rivals is neither here nor there for the moment however Brenda. The damage is already done! What concerns me now is to take steps to protect my business affairs from any future possibility of a repetition. One possibility I have considered is to release Roger from his position within my firm. At least by doing so I would guard myself from any further damage caused by his wife's imbecilic and garrulous tongue!"

Brenda gazed at him in shock. "Sir! My Lord! I...I implore you! Please don't fire Roger. I... I know I was foolish but I... I swear that it will not happen again." Brenda dabbed at her eyes with a napkin.

Lord Castlebridge dismissed her pleading with a snort. "Young lady I will require much greater assurances than merely your grovelling apologies and a few tears of sorrow. I shall demand a much sterner measure of your contrition than that! In fact I will go so far as to say that Roger's continued employment with the company is entirely conditional upon your agreeing to the measures I have in mind and by demonstrating your remorse in your actions by submitting yourself to them."

Brenda's face paled almost to the hue of the linen napkin she was applying to her tears. "W...what measures?" she asked in a feeble whisper.

Lord Castlebridge ignored her and turned to Roger. "You are as much to blame for all this as well Roger. Your wife is a lady who should have been administered with a firm hand right from the beginning. Instead you let things slip; turned a blind eye to her folly and indiscretion. I expect better from my executives. If a man cannot deal with his own domestic affairs with firm decisiveness how can I expect him to demonstrate those qualities in his professional capacity? If you are to continue in my employ then I wish to see hard evidence that you are prepared to exercise the firm disciplinary measures your wife so clearly is in need of."

Roger nodded. "Yes Sir."

"Well?"

"Well what sir?"

"Are you and your wife prepared to accept the consequences of your wife's actions and hereby agree to whatever corrective measures I deem fit or do you wish to take your services elsewhere."

Roger glanced at his wife nervously. "I... I mean we both will agree to any measures you feel necessary sir."

Lord Castlebridge turned sharply to Brenda. "And you young lady? Will you also agree to the measures I have decided upon? Remember that your husband's employment and your continued prosperity depend upon it."

Brenda nodded abjectly. "Y...yes sir." She took a deep breath. "What measures do you propose sir?"

"I am going to have you punished Brenda; severely punished in such a fashion as to teach you a lesson for once and for all!" His Lordship turned back to Roger. "And as for you Roger I not only expect you to agree to your wife's punishment but I also expect you to witness it and take example from it so as to know in future exactly how I expect you to deal with your wife in any similar circumstances in the future."

Roger glanced sharply at his wife who was weeping softly on the other side of the table. He knew in that instance that his career held by a hair's breadth. He felt suddenly angry that his wife's idiocy had brought them to this. He took a long measured breath. "I will agree to whatever you say

My Lord." He stared at the glass in front of him; the fine cognac in it now forgotten. "What punishment do you have in mind sir?"

Lord Castlebridge rose from his seat. "If you'd like to follow me I can best show you that. Brenda you will accompany us, and Greenwood, you as well if you please." He paused before turning to his wife. "Cynthia I'd like you to witness this as well. Bring your two girls along too. They may be of some assistance."

Lord Castlebridge led the solemn procession out of the dining room and along the corridors of the Hall. Brenda tripped along fearfully in the centre of the group wondering feverishly what "punishment" might be in store for her. Walking sympathetically at her side Lady Castlebridge had no doubt whatsoever what was in store for her friend. Their path was leading inexorably toward the library. Brenda's nemesis awaited her there. Lady Castlebridge felt truly sorry for her.

CHAPTER 13

"This, Roger, is the caning stool." Lord Castlebridge announced with satisfaction, patting the polished oak surface of the intimidating item of furniture with something approaching affectionate pride. They were in the library, of course, and the cavernous, high ceilinged room, its walls filled with bookshelves, busts and portraits of the Hall's illustrious family heritage was, following the completion of the repairs, back to it's customary condition of pristine orderliness. The furniture in here was solid and robust in contrast to the more ornate and fussy styles to be found elsewhere in the Hall; massive oak writing tables, desks and chairs. There was no place for frivolity in this great chamber. It was a room dedicated to serious and sombre study and education. It served as the private schoolroom for the generations of the Hall's children and study chamber for its adults. All the Hall's archives and family records were kept in here and all significant events were soberly recorded into the massive tomes which served as the living history of Castlebridge Hall.

It was natural therefore that such a serious and imposing chamber would have also become the room in which the disciplinary requirements of the Hall were conducted. Disciplinary inquiries or hearings were carried out at a massive long table big enough to accommodate a committee of senior staff members or representatives of the Hall's dynasty facing a solitary chair upon which generations of miscreants had seated themselves to face the charges against them and answer for their behaviour. Many a deliberation had been performed at that table and many a trembling culprit ordered to stand to hear the resultant verdict and have sentence passed upon them.

Not only would the cowering delinquent hear their fate in that chamber but, as the place where traditionally their sentence was executed, it was also well equipped to carry out the punishments deemed appropriate to the crimes of the wrong-doers unfortunate to face the penalties for their misdeeds in that intimidating chamber. In a clear space at one end of the enormous room, often threatened but seldom used, was the whipping stand; the chains from the ceiling ending in solid leather cuffs to secure the wrists and stretch up the arms of anybody whose misdeeds were of sufficient seriousness to warrant the use of the long whip across their wretched body.

At the far end of the room was the birching post: the short stake, with a horizontal cross beam at the top of it, rising from a raised dais to which the guilty would be firmly affixed in a kneeling position to receive a birching. The birching post had somewhat fallen into disfavour in recent times in the Hall's armoury of disciplinary measures but the good sound birching of Charlotte Carlton and her three cohorts in idle negligence had once again established a precedent for the use of this highly efficacious means of correction. It was now a firm opinion of Lord Castlebridge and his butler, Greenwood, that the public birching of the four young ladies had had such an admirably immediate effect in the immediate raising of standards of diligent hard work since, that the birching post had justified its more regular employment for the maintenance of those standards.

Holding pride of place in the centre of the chamber however was the most commonly used item of disciplinary furniture; the caning stool, to which His Lordship now directed Roger Brideshead's attention. Roger stood and stared at the stern and solid artefact in fascination. It was clearly venerable and, judging by its smooth worn surface, it must have seen much usage down the long years of its history. It was a massive frame built of solid oak timber and bolted back into place, securely to the wooden parquet of the library floor. The broad leather strap with its buckles lying across the concave surface of the stool looked ancient but well maintained as did the shorter straps attached to the four solid legs of the stool. Bizarrely Roger wondered whose responsibility in the Hall it was to regularly come into this chamber to oil the straps and polish the brass buckles on this forbidding item of the household's furniture. In his mind's eye Roger envisaged the generations of penitents who must have found themselves strapped down to this awful apparatus for failing to live up to the exacting standards of this ancient house and its revered traditions.

Almost as if reading his thoughts, Lord Castlebridge patted the stool once more and continued. "Yes Roger the caning stool! It has a long history in this house. You might say that the character and backbone of our family heritage were forged and built on the foundations of this single heirloom of our past. The first Lord of Castlebridge had this constructed and installed in here shortly after the acquisition of the Hall back in the sixteenth century. It has been a perpetual rock of family tradition ever since. Newer, more up to date, disciplinary measures have had their vogue at various times over the centuries but the old caning stool has remained a constant; an unwavering reminder to all within these walls of the duties and responsibilities expected of all those who live and serve under this roof and the consequences of failing to do so. This is the stone upon which this house is built!"

Roger tore his eyes away from the stool for a second to glance at his wife. She was cowering against the wall of the library; her face white with fear and her lips trembling, the significance of Lord Castlebridge's words not lost on her, and she was staring in mesmerised horror at the object His Lordship was so proudly displaying. Lady Castlebridge had an arm around Brenda's shoulder in sympathetic comfort while the two young maids of Her Ladyship stood in pale faced attendance. Greenwood stood austerely to one side bearing a silver tray upon which resided the cognac decanter. Presumably he had felt that the gentlemen would require some fortifying refreshment whilst obliged to attend to the disagreeable duty that was so obviously now in the offing.

Roger dragged his attention back to Lord Castlebridge. "Really sir?" he mumbled hastily. "That... that sounds very interesting."

Lord Castlebridge nodded sagely. "Yes Roger; a proud old tradition of my family. The caning stool is no mere antiquity however: no curiosity from the mists of time. It, and the other disciplinary items you see in this room, are still regularly employed to correct misbehaviour within this house and to serve as a constant deterrent to the misconduct of all who reside here. Nor is its usage confined to the staff and servants of this house. Members of the family are expected to live up to the same standards of behaviour and responsibility imposed upon those within the family employ and, if they fail to do so, can expect to make the acquaintance of this stool in their turn."

Lord Castlebridge paused to sip at his cognac. "Indeed Roger I would have it no other way. Members of the family have, after all, a duty to set an example of conduct worthy of this house to the lower members of the house and, should they be found lacking in that duty, it is only fitting that they be seen to endure the same consequences which even the lowliest minion in service can expect." Lord Castlebridge nodded briefly in the direction of the little huddled group against the wall. "I can tell you Roger that not even my own wife is immune from such consequences. Why only this week it was my duty to have her strapped to this very stool and caned for her foolishness at Ascot last week."

Roger was astonished by this intelligence. He glanced at Lady Castlebridge who had blushed crimson and lowered her eyes in shame. "You... you had y... your...I mean Lady Castlebridge caned?" stammered Roger in bewilderment.

Lord Castlebridge nodded gravely. “Yes indeed Roger! She foolishly squandered seven thousand pounds on the horses at damn Ascot and so I thought it best to teach her a lesson for her profligacy.”

Roger shook his head disbelievingly and reached out to finger the smooth worn leather of the waist strap on the caning stool. “And you had her strapped to... to this in here sir?”

Lord Castlebridge shook his head. “Not exactly Roger. As chance would have it we had workmen in the library that day so Greenwood carried out the punishment in his pantry. The caning stool was temporarily installed in Greenwood's pantry should its use be required while the library was out of commission.”

Roger blinked in increasing astonishment at this further information. “Are you saying that you had your butler cane Her Ladyship sir?”

“Yes that’s right Roger. Greenwood is excellent with the cane and other implements; very precise and with a firm hand. I use his talents for most of the discipline in the Hall; my strong right arm you might say.”

“You astound me My Lord!”

“Quite Roger. I tell you this in order to impress upon you that I demand just as exacting a code of conduct from my own wife as I expect you to impose upon yours and, equally, I am just as prepared to discipline her in the same way that I will require you to deal with your own wife’s misconduct.”

Roger swallowed. “I....I see sir.”

Lord Castlebridge regarded him sternly and lifted a finger in admonition. “Yes Roger and I’m bound to say that, had you had an equally firm policy, then the events that have brought us to this would have been very unlikely to occur. Were there a similar device to this installed in your own house, and you were prepared to use it when needed, then I have to say that it is highly improbable that we would have lost such lucrative business through your wife’s foolish indiscretion. A short sharp lesson over such a device, when she first demonstrated this propensity of hers for idle, foolish chatter, and we would not have seen it escalate to the level of seriousness it has become. I cannot impress this upon you strongly enough. Do you take my meaning young man?”

Roger blushed but nodded humbly. “Yes sir.”

“This evening is not just intended as a lesson to your wife Roger but also as a lesson to yourself! The measures that I intend to see carried out this evening are measures that I will expect you to introduce into your own domestic arrangements and ensure that they are fully adhered to in the future. Is that perfectly clear?”

Roger nodded penitently once more. “Yes sir.”

“Excellent! Now to practicalities. Before we commence with the main business in hand, I’d like to demonstrate the functioning of this stool so that you will see how it is utilised when such time arrives that you install a similar device in your own home.” Lord Castlebridge cast his eye thoughtfully over the group of women huddled together by the wall. His eye fell on the two young personal maids of his wife. He raised his finger and pointed at Suzette. "You young lady. Would you kindly step over here for a moment?"

Suzette paled in sudden fear. For a moment Roger thought her legs were going to give way beneath her. "'Oo me My Lord?" she whispered in shock.

"Yes you young lady! Quick as you can if you please."

Suzette bit her lip to stifle the groan that threatened to escape from her mouth and paced forward, her legs trembling. "Oui My Lord." she responded in a fearful whisper.

"Yes would you mount the caning stool please young lady?"

"Ze... ze caning st... stool My Lord?" Suzette stuttered in dread.

"That is correct! Come along young lady. I'm sure you know the correct procedure. It's not the first time you've had to present yourself at the caning stool, as both you and I know!" Terrified, Suzette stepped up onto the box positioned at the front of the stool. "You'll note Roger that the young lady is obliged to stand on the box placed for convenience there before bending over the stool." Lord Castlebridge observed conversationally. "The stool is rather too high for the young ladies of the house and it is important that they position themselves so that the top of the stool is level with their hips before bending over to present themselves for the cane. Carry on please Suzette." With a tiny whimper and, with the tears pricking at her eyes, Suzette leaned forward to drape herself over the stool. Lord Castlebridge nodded in satisfaction. "Now this is the correct position for the young lady to adopt before being secured Roger. You'll see that she is standing on tip toe to prostrate herself over the stool and her tummy is lying firmly in the indented surface of it. Now once she is secured with the straps and the box removed, her centre of gravity will be firmly in the middle of the stool and her feet clear of the floor. Now if you will assist me Roger."

Lord Castlebridge moved to the Suzette's side and gesturing to Roger to take up a position at the opposite side of the stool. "If you would pass me the strap over please Roger?"

"Yes sir." Roger handed the broad leather strap over Suzette's midriff. Lord Castlebridge passed the tip through the buckle on his side and tightened the strap firmly before fastening it securely.

"You want the waist strap to be firm and secure Roger. It shouldn't be too tight as to squeeze the breath out of her but firm enough to hold her belly securely against the surface of the stool and to push her bottom up nicely for the cane."

Roger was becoming interested in proceedings. The pretty little girl, trembling in her fetching maid's uniform, looked so helpless and forlorn strapped down across the stool that he felt a quickening of erotic arousal at the sight. Feigning dispassionate interest, he ran a finger under the leather strap to test the firmness of the bonding. There was just enough give in the strap to wriggle a finger between it and the softness of the girl's uniform. He could feel the warmth of her body through the thin material and felt her shiver at his touch. "I see sir. And the next step?"

"The next step is to secure her wrists with the straps on the front legs Roger. I shall fasten this side if you will attend to the one on yours. Once again make sure her wrists are firmly held but not so tight as to cut off the circulation to her hands." Roger squatted at the front of the young girl to take her hand gently but firmly and buckle her right wrist into the strap affixed to the front leg. He glanced at her face, inches away from his. She was staring at him abjectly, her eyes wild with fear and damp with tears. He felt an almost over powering urge to reach out and stroke her face. He took a deep breath and averted his gaze.

"Now, if you're all done on that side Roger, we next need to secure her legs." Roger rose from his squatting position and joined Lord Castlebridge behind the girl. "Now this is the crucial and most tricky part Roger." His Lordship warned. "You have to lift her leg away from the box and pull it over to the stool leg to fasten the strap. If she's in the right position you'll find that the strap fastens around her lower calf just above the knee. You'll probably have to lift her dress slightly out of the way to facilitate passing the strap around her leg."

Roger squatted down to follow the instructions. He pushed the hem of her dress, and the frilly petticoat beneath, out of the way to take hold of her leg. Suzette wore no stockings. The bare flesh of her thigh was silky and maddeningly enticing to his touch. His heart was pounding in his chest and once again he felt her shudder at the touch of his fingers on the bare skin at the back of her thighs. Slowly and deliberately he pulled her leg to the side and passed the leather strap around it, letting his hand linger a second on the warm flesh before buckling the strap. Lord Castlebridge completed preparations on the other leg and rose to survey the results. Almost reluctantly, Roger followed suit, rising to his feet and trying to control his breathing.

Lord Castlebridge seemed satisfied. "There now Roger. That's just about right. Now her legs are spread apart and her feet clear of the ground. All her weight is now on her tummy in the middle of the stool and she's firmly held in position to receive her punishment." Lord Castlebridge stepped forward and lifted Suzette's dress and petticoat, to raise them above her waist and lay them across her prone back. Roger felt his mouth dry as the action exposed the entire length of the girl's thighs and her pert rounded bottom covered only by the thin material of her lacy knickers. He thought at that moment he had never seen anything more alluring.

Lord Castlebridge however, seemed more concerned with practical demonstration rather than the erotic display of the young girl's charming nether portions. He patted Suzette lightly on the rump and Roger saw the girl flinch at the contact. "Now this is how the bottom should be presented Roger. The caning stool is used primarily for corporal punishment on the buttocks and the backs of the thighs. You can see how the girl's bottom is admirably thrust out and firmly held in position to be caned and how her legs are held securely to apply the cane to the sensitive regions on the upper thighs as well." Lord Castlebridge paused to finish the last drops of his cognac. "Of course, were this a formal punishment, in the ordinary course of events, this young lady would have been obliged to remove her knickers or perhaps disrobe completely before being strapped down to the stool. Canings and other punishments are most usually administered to the bare bottom in this house." His Lordship patted Suzette's bottom once more with an affectionate smile. "However since this is just a demonstration we will spare the young lady's blushes!"

Roger felt almost disappointed but he could feel an almost physical wave of relief emanating from the girl over the caning stool. Her embarrassment was not to be spared entirely however for Lord Castlebridge laid his glass aside and marched around to her front. He raised her face with his fingertips under her chin and looked her in the eye. "Now Suzette you are entirely familiar with this position ate you not?"

The young maid nodded miserably. "Oui monsieur."

"Perhaps you would care to remind us when it was the last time you found yourself over this stool."

"S'il vous plait Monsieur, eet was in Janvier just after ze New Year."

"Yes. And what was your punishment on that occasion?"

"I... I 'ave given fifty strokes Monsieur."

Lord Castlebridge nodded in satisfaction. "Precisely! Perhaps you would tell Mr Brideshead here for just what offence you were awarded such a severe punishment."

Suzette blushed and seemed ready to burst into tears. "Eet was for ze drunkenness Monsieur." she murmured abjectly.

His Lordship nodded once more. "Yes Roger. This little madam drank herself silly on New Year's Eve and made a complete disgrace of herself. She wasn't alone in this." His Lordship nodded at Maria who was currently trying unsuccessfully to blend into the woodwork. "That young lady there was also guilty although her behaviour was not quite as disgraceful as this one's and I believe she received a lesser sentence." Lord Castlebridge paused thoughtfully. "Ordinarily, given the festive nature of the season, I might have been inclined to be lenient with alcoholic over indulgence had it been an isolated case. Sadly that was not the case however. There had been a number of occasions when this young lady and, to a lesser extent, her colleague had, I'm afraid to say, displayed behaviour of this nature. I was becoming concerned about it Roger and had the occasion to discuss the matter with my wife two or three times, since these young ladies are her personal maids. I hate to see young lives ruined by alcohol dependency so, when there was a repetition on New Year's Eve, I decided to act and had the pair of them marched in here for a flogging!"

Lord Castlebridge turned his attention back to the unhappy Suzette. "So young lady! You received fifty strokes. Did it teach you a lesson?"

Suzette nodded hastily. "Ah oui Monsieur."

"And have you been drinking since?"

Suzette shook her head vigorously. “Ah non! Pas une goutte Monsieur!” Suzette's protestation of innocence was not entirely candid but, since she and Maria had been caned for drunken wantoness on New Years Eve, they had been careful to confine their drinking to those times when they were well away from the Hall or to the privacy of the attic room they shared under the eaves of the house above their Mistress's chambers.

Lord Castlebridge tucked his thumbs into his waistcoat pockets and rocked back on his heels in satisfaction. “I rest my case Roger! There you have it in a nutshell! That was, what, six months ago? Here was a young lady on the slippery slope to drunken wastage; a possible young life ruined by the temptations of the bottle and what is the solution? Why a few minutes labour with the cane for Greenwood, six months later a reformed young lady and not a drop has passed her lips since: simple, effective and to the point!”

Roger conceded the point. “Yes sir.”

“And that Roger is what you should have done when your own wife’s tipsy flirting first led her into dangerous indiscretions. Had you acted firmly with her even six months ago we would not find ourselves in the situation we are in now.”

“No sir.”

A look of stern resolution crossed Lord Castlebridge’s face. “Well hopefully Roger it is not too late to make amends and correct matters.” He turned to the other of Her Ladyship’s personal maids. “Maria would you step over here a moment?”

The young girl complied nervously. “Yes My Lord?”

“I might as well say this whilst you are both present. I’ve been generally pleased with your behaviour this year since you were both caned and my wife seems satisfied with your service. However I have noticed a tendency of late for the pair of you to be somewhat over familiar with both myself and my wife. I don’t want the pair of you to feel that because you are obliged to attend to Her Ladyship’s intimate personal needs that it permits you such a degree of familiarity.”

Lady Castlebridge froze her face into a mask at these words. This was dangerous territory. She was fairly certain that her pompous husband perfectly aware of the extent of her “personal needs” but she made a mental note to exercise more caution in future, in any case, and counsel her two maids to do the same.

“I want you two young ladies to remember your place.” His Lordship continued. “Now I’m not going to have you caned on this occasion.” There was an audible gasp of relief from Suzette, still firmly secured, prostrate over the caning stool, with her dress above her waist. Lord Castlebridge ignored it and expounded further. “I do however serve you both due warning. I expect to see a little more deference and respect in future or you will both be renewing your acquaintance with this item of furniture. Do I make myself plain?” The two girls intoned their affirmations in unison. “Excellent!” continued Lord Castlebridge, “Now Maria you may release your companion.”

Lord Castlebridge turned to his butler. "Oh Greenwood I wonder if you'd be so good as to refresh Mr Brideshead's glass and I'll have another drop too."

"Very good My Lord."

"Capital. Now Roger if you'll step over here I'd like to show you the tools we use for the job." His Lordship took Roger's arm and led him to a cupboard set in the wall. He flung the doors open to reveal an intimidating array of disciplinary instruments hanging from hooks within. Lord Castlebridge reached out to finger the items on display. "Now these are the canes we use Roger. You'll see that they are all around five to six feet long. Greenwood's a strong believer in long canes. He asserts that you get a much better swing and subsequently firmer impact with a longer cane and I have to say I agree with him. You'll also note that they are not too thin. Greenwood can't be doing with thin canes. They sting somewhat it is true but they don't have the weight to strike with real authority. He doesn't advocate very thick canes either however because they don't have the same bite. A good cane should be a compromise between a concentrated striking area and sufficient weight to deliver the stroke firmly within that area. I find, and Greenwood concurs with my opinion, that around a quarter of an inch or a little over half a centimetre thick to be ideal."

Greenwood was at their side. "Your drinks My Lord."

"Ah thank you Greenwood." Lord Castlebridge took his cognac before continuing. "You'll see that we use other implements than the cane as well Roger. The leather straps and tawses here are generally for lesser punishments and the whips you see are for very serious offences, apart from those multi thonged affairs which are called martinets. We use those for lighter whippings on the bottom, bare back or other parts of the anatomy."

"You mentioned a birching post earlier sir. Do you not keep the birches in this cupboard?"

Lord Castlebridge sipped at his cognac and shook his head. "No Roger. We've only just reintroduced birching for serious offences but there is a certain long tradition concerning the birch in our family that stretches back generations. A person who is to be birched is obliged to walk down to the woods on the estate and cut the birch twigs themselves and bind them together to fashion the birch switch to be used on them. It was formerly conceived as a way to emphasise the person's acknowledgement of their guilt by making them contribute to the process of their own punishment. I see no reason to change a tried and trusted old method and so we stick to the old tradition. Fearful anticipation of one's forthcoming punishment is, after all, part and parcel of the whole disciplinary process and anyone who has to walk down to the woods to make their own birch switch will have plenty of time to reflect upon their misconduct and dread the consequences of it."

"I see sir. Yes I can understand how that would reinforce the message somewhat."

"Exactly. Anyway enough of the lecture for the time being. I think it's about time to turn to the business in hand."

Lord Castlebridge turned back to the caning stool, now divested of Suzette's prostrate form through the ministrations of Maria. Suzette was now back against the wall alongside her mistress, smoothing out the creases in her dress and looking thoroughly relieved. She had been sure that she was for the cane. Brenda however was looking anything but comforted. His Lordship's words concerning the beneficent advantages of allowing the culprit time to reflect upon the ordeal awaiting them would have struck a chord of recognition in the young woman whose fear was rising by the second.

Lord Castlebridge fixed her with a look of grim reproach that brooked no protest. "Brenda! Would you oblige me by stepping into the centre of the room please?"

In mounting trepidation Brenda stepped forward although it seemed to her as if her legs were not working properly and threatening to give way beneath her. She came to a halt a few feet from His Lordship and stood there clasping her hands in agitation and her face white with foreboding. There was a pause for several seconds as Lord Castlebridge regarded her sternly. "Well," he said at last, "I think you know by now why you're here young lady and what is in store for you. Do you have anything to say for yourself?"

Brenda's vocal chords seemed to be suffering a similar malady of malfunction as her legs and for several seconds she tried desperately to articulate. When she at last found voice it was only to murmur a feeble apology. Lord Castlebridge was not impressed. “I think we covered all this over the dinner table Brenda. Your apologies have been deemed insufficient to compensate for your foolishness. We agreed then, you, your husband and I that you deserved to be punished. Do you see any justification in modifying that evaluation now that you better understand the nature of the punishment awaiting you?”

Brenda’s eyes kept flicking in torment between Lord Castlebridge and the caning stool. She was gripped by a sense of dreadful unreality; as if this nightmare must be happening to somebody else. She just couldn’t believe that His Lordship truly intended to strap her to that infernal contraption and have her beaten. It had to be some terrible mistake. “Well Brenda? I am waiting. Have you lost your tongue?”

“N...no My Lord. I... I....” Brenda tailed off unable to express herself or plead for mercy.”

“I see that you have nothing to offer in mitigation therefore we will proceed. Well I’m afraid you *are* going to be punished Brenda; severely punished. You are to be taught a lesson this evening Brenda and one which I sincerely hope will stay with you for a long time to come. If you have nothing further to say I would be obliged if you prepared yourself for punishment now.”

Brenda stared at him in shock. “In...in w... what way sir?” she stammered.

“By disrobing Brenda...completely!”

Brenda stared at him in shock. “I’m sorry?”

“I said by disrobing Brenda. I require you to get undressed!”

"You... you mean... take my clothes off?"

"I do indeed young lady... all of them if you please!"

"Take *all* my clothes off?" Brenda squeaked disbelievingly.

Lord Castlebridge's patience was wearing thin. "Good heavens young lady! Are my instructions so difficult to follow? Of course I mean you to remove *all* your clothes. You are to be punished naked! You may regard your loss of dignity and modesty as part of the penance imposed on you and a little humiliation is good for the soul, I always say."

Brenda glanced toward her husband for support but she found little sympathy there. "Do as you're told Brenda." he commanded her quietly but firmly.

Lord Castlebridge turned to his wife's young maids. "Will you two girls assist Mrs Brideshead please?"

The two girls curtsied and stepped forward. "Yes My Lord." They took up station on either side of Brenda. "We'll hold your clothes ma'am." Maria told her sympathetically.

"So if you please young lady." Lord Castlebridge urged her. "I would be obliged if you complied with the orders you have been given."

Trapped by the inevitable, Brenda had run out of alternatives. She choked back a sob and, with trembling fingers, began to unbutton her blouse. The silence in the room was heavy and pregnant as she fumbled despairingly with the buttons, broken only by the soft whimpering that escaped her throat and the rustle of the fabric of her blouse. In deep humiliation she slipped her blouse from her shoulders. Suzette took the garment from her gently and folded it neatly before placing it carefully on a nearby table.

Brenda had trouble with the zip on the back of her skirt. Perhaps her fingers were trembling too hard to manipulate the awkward fastener or perhaps it was just that it became stuck. Whatever the reason, Maria was obliged to assist her, squatting down behind her to work the zipper and helping Brenda slip her skirt off her hips, down her legs and free of her ankles. Placing the folded skirt over the crook of her arm, from her position at Brenda's feet, Maria looked up with sympathy at the frightened half naked woman. "I'd best take your shoes as well ma'am." she told her. Brenda nodded miserably and Maria provided a comforting shoulder for her to rest a hand as she raised each foot, in turn, for the young maid to take her shoes.

Lord Castlebridge approved of Brenda's underwear. He liked to see his ladies in attractive feminine undergarments and Brenda's ensemble of matching bra and knickers in soft pink with white trimmings was eminently fetching on the young woman's admirably trim body. As Maria rose to her feet clutching Brenda's skirt and shoes, he nodded to her companion. "Would you take Mrs Brideshead's jewellery for her please Suzette?"

He turned to Roger. "I usually prefer to have ladies take off their jewellery before punishment Roger." he remarked by way of explanation. "Bangles and wristwatches get in the way when securing their wrists and I'm always cautious that necklaces may get broken or, worse yet, become entangled as they struggle in their bonds and cause choking. Also, it may be a small point, but there is always the possibility of small, but valuable, items of jewellery becoming detached and lost as they squirm about under the pain of their punishment. Better to be safe, I always think. A lady doesn't need her pretty little decorations while she's having her bottom thrashed!"

"No sir." mumbled Roger in agreement as he watched Suzette divest his wife of her jewellery; her bracelet and wristwatch, her necklace, her diamond earrings and even her wedding ring. Brenda it seemed would have to take her punishment in no other adornments than those that nature had provided her with.

Yet Brenda herself seemed reluctant to accept that her total nudity was required for punishment. She stood there miserably in her underwear, reluctant to shed these last wispy tokens of her modesty. Lord Castlebridge frowned at her. "And the rest if you please young lady." he urged her firmly. With a tiny sob, Brenda reached behind to unfasten her bra. Having removed this item she clasped a hand across her breasts timidly. This made it awkward to take off her knickers with one hand and once again Maria was obliged to aid her by squatting down to pull her knickers down her legs and clear of her feet as Brenda clasped her other hand over her sex.

Now completely naked, Brenda huddled abjectly, trying to cover her modesty with her hands. This did not meet Lord Castlebridge's approval. "Stand up straight girl!" he commanded her "And put your hands behind your head." With a sob of pathetic dismay Brenda complied with painful slowness. Once she had assumed the required position, Lord Castlebridge took the opportunity to take a long appraisal of the naked young woman. On the whole he liked what he saw. It was easy enough, he knew, to look attractive with a budget that allowed one to bedeck oneself in fine clothes but Brenda was splendid looking young lady with her clothes off as well. She was slim yet with perfectly proportioned curves, pert firm breasts and buttocks, long slender legs and her glorious, long, dark, wavy hair fell down over shapely, trim shoulders. She was in fact a remarkably beautiful young woman. Little wonder that the half the young studs in the county came sniffing around her at social events! Well, after the lesson she was about to take, it was likely that she'd be a little more circumspect in her dealings with them in future!

His Lordship turned to Roger approvingly. "I must compliment you Roger. You have a fine figure of a wife."

"Thank you sir."

Lord Castlebridge returned his gaze to the trembling Brenda. "Turn around girl. Let me look at you properly." Withering under His Lordship's appraisal, Brenda turned around slowly. Lord Castlebridge grunted appreciatively. "Yes, most pleasant Roger." he affirmed. There was one slight flaw in Roger's wife that His Lordship might have taken issue with. She was rather too bushy in the pubic regions for his tastes. Lord Castlebridge had, as has been noted, somewhat of a bee in his bonnet regarding pubic hair. Not only did he regard it as unsightly but he was also of the firm opinion that it was unhygienic. As a result of this peculiar obsession of his, every female in the house was obliged to shave her pubic hair regularly and it was not at all uncommon for His Lordship to demand of some young maid that she lower her knickers for examination to see whether his wishes were being carried out in this respect. Lord Castlebridge was a stickler in this matter and few among the household maids dared risk the consequences of a spot check. Nevertheless, he held his peace in this instance since it was Roger's affair, after all, how he wished his wife to present herself naked. It might even be possible that he liked his wife a little hirsute in that part of her anatomy and it wasn't his business to criticise it.

Shaking the thoughts from his mind, Lord Castlebridge turned his attention once more to immediate business. "Well young lady we haven't come here to admire your womanly attributes, charming though they may be. You are here to be punished!" He turned to address his butler. "Greenwood. Would you be so kind as to select a suitable cane please?"

"Of course My Lord." Greenwood stepped over to the cabinet on the far wall.

A loud sob escaped Brenda's lips at the word "cane" and Lord Castlebridge looked at her sharply. "Yes that's right young lady! You heard correctly. You are to be caned! There's no point sulking about it now. You deserve everything you've got coming to you so you'll just have to put up and bear it!"

“Would this implement be suitable do you think My Lord?” asked Greenwood, holding out a cane inquiringly.

Lord Castlebridge held out a hand. “Let’s have a look Greenwood.” He took the cane and examined it carefully. He approved almost immediately of Greenwood’s choice. It was the longest cane in the cabinet, a regulation quarter of an inch thick, admirably weighted and sound with a fashioned suede covered handle on one end to facilitate a firm grip. “Capital Greenwood! Just the job!”

He turned to Brenda who was regarding the terrible instrument with hypnotised horror. “Yes take a good long look young lady! You’re going to be feeling this across your rear end all too soon. This is the price of your foolishness and your dalliance with young suitors. A married woman has no business flirting with young men in the first place, let alone divulging her husband’s confidential business dealings to them. Well you’ll be singing a different tune very shortly! Now if you would be so kind, please step up to the caning stool for the administration of your punishment.” Lord Castlebridge nodded to Maria and Suzette. “Would you two girls assist Mrs Brideshead please and show her the correct position to take before strapping her down. Greenwood I’d be obliged if you’d supervise and make sure the girls strap her in properly.”

“Yes My Lord.”

Brenda thought for one awful moment that her bladder would disgrace her as she stepped forward to the caning stool. She felt slightly dizzy and faint, and the sounds in the room seemed to echo as if from far away; hollow and unconnected to reality. In a daze she stepped gingerly in her bare feet onto the box and, with the two girls' guidance, leaned forward over the terrible stool. She felt the cool leather of the strap across the back of her waist as Maria passed it across to her companion and then her stomach pressed firmly against the hard surface of the stool as Suzette tightened it in the buckle. "Your hand please ma'am." murmured Maria softly and Brenda let her take her arm and stared almost in incomprehension at the girl fastening the strap around her slender wrist. Suzette attended to her other wrist. Brenda tried to move her arms but they were firmly secured to the legs of the stool.

Then the girls moved to her rear. Brenda felt their hands upon her legs and the tips of her toes lost their final contact with the box as they lifted and parted her thighs to secure them to the back legs. She felt shamefully exposed as the girls tightened the straps on her thighs. Her bottom was thrust out invitingly for the cane in Lord Castlebridge's hand and, with her legs parted, her sex was displayed disgracefully to everyone in the room. She gripped the legs of the stool with her bound hands and stared fixedly ahead with a quivering lip as Greenwood examined the straps; her face burning with humiliation and shame.

Once Greenwood had expressed his satisfaction with the girls' work in binding Brenda to the stool, Lord Castlebridge turned to Roger. "Roger, with your permission, I'd like Greenwood to administer your wife's caning. He's the expert here and I trust him to do a thorough job. Would that be all right with you?"

Roger swallowed. He had watched his wife strip naked and be strapped into the caning stool with mesmerised fascination. The eroticism of Suzette's bondage to the caning stool had been surpassed by the sight of his naked wife suspended and bound over the same apparatus. He was uncomfortably aware of the urgent throbbing from the bulge in his trousers. Hastily he cleared his throat. "Yes sir. Quite all right." His voice sounded unnaturally high to him.

"Good! In that case Greenwood it's all yours." Lord Castlebridge handed the cane back to his butler before addressing Roger once more. "Of course Roger there will be times to come when you will need to discipline your own wife in future, therefore I advise you to watch carefully and observe Greenwood's technique so as best to apply it when it is necessary to do the job yourself."

"Yes sir. Of course sir."

"Excellent. I think you will find it most instructive. Very well Greenwood. You may proceed."

Greenwood gave a small cough. "Er forgive me My Lord but you have not yet specified the number of strokes Mrs Brideshead is to receive. Would you care to clarify that My Lord?"

"Ah yes of course. Sorry Greenwood. Forgetful of me! Would you administer one hundred strokes please?" There was a strangled gasp of horrified protest from the waiting Brenda. Lord Castlebridge frowned at her. "You might well squeak young lady but it is nothing less than you deserve! I intend you to learn a lesson you will never forget!" His Lordship turned to Roger. "I know it may seem a severe sentence to impose upon your wife Roger but I consider it appropriate to the seriousness of her offence. Once again I must point out that had you taken firmer steps with her earlier she might have spared herself the severity of the caning due to her by her reformed behaviour. However, since you took no such steps, then her conduct has deteriorated to the point where nothing less severe will suffice to match the gravity of her dereliction. I presume you agree with me."

Roger nodded in a slight daze. "Yes sir. I bow to your better judgement in the matter sir."

"Capital. In that case, let us continue. Carry on if you would Greenwood."

"Very good sir." There was an awful, expectant hush as Greenwood removed his jacket with great dignity and rolled up his shirt sleeve. In some ways Castlebridge Hall's butler seemed even more imposing without his jacket on; the solid width of his powerful shoulders bulging at his shirt and waistcoat. With quiet, dignified efficiency he picked up the cane and stepped forward to address Brenda's quivering posterior. Tiny moans of despair from the trembling young lady were the only sounds to break the tense silence as Greenwood measured the distance and raised the cane high above his shoulder. Then, in a terrible whistling blur, the cane arced through its swing directly into the centre of Brenda's buttocks.

Lady Castlebridge and her two maids flinched

and visibly cringed at the loud whoosh of the cane punctuated by the sharp crack as it bit into the orbs of Brenda's bottom. Their reaction was nothing however in comparison to the unfortunate recipient of that awful first stroke. Brenda's body jerked violently under the solid impact of the cane, her eyes flew open in shock and the sudden pain that exploded in her rear drove a loud cry from her lungs. Brenda had expected the cane to hurt of course but nothing had prepared her for the scorching concentration of agony from that first stroke. As Greenwood lifted the cane once more the pain of the first stroke seemed to spread across her bottom and penetrate deep into the muscle. She closed her eyes tightly and gritted her teeth against its welling intensity.

Suzette bit her lip in sympathy as she watched Brenda struggle with the torment of that first stroke. The fifty strokes she had received from Greenwood in January had been probably the most wretched experience of her young life. She was a little vague as to exactly what Brenda's offence had been but it must have been something truly spectacular to earn her a hundred strokes. Suzette shivered at the very thought. Her companion Maria was equally sympathetic. She remembered feelingly the first time she had ever had to undergo a caning. She recalled her own shock at the terrible pain of the first stroke and the awful awareness that it was only the first of many. Her sentence on that first occasion had been thirty strokes and she remembered her despair at the thought of another twenty nine equally agonising ones to follow. For this poor woman there were another ninety nine to face. She must be in a truly terrible place by now.

Greenwood lifted the cane to deliver the second stroke but before he could administer it Lord Castlebridge raised a hand. "One moment if you please Greenwood. I'd like Roger to see this." His Lordship directed Roger's attention to the crimson stripe now appearing on his wife's bottom. "Now that's how a mark from the cane should look like Roger." His Lordship pointed out. "Clear, defined and parallel to the ground. You'll note that Greenwood doesn't flick at the target or allow the cane to bounce off but delivers it firmly and with plenty of follow through to bite deeply into the flesh. A well delivered stroke should leave a good, clear welt with exact precision on the bottom."

Roger peered at the single line of the cane across his wife's bottom with interest ignoring the gasping sobs from his wife. "I see sir."

Lord Castlebridge nodded. "Yes Roger. Greenwood's great skill is in landing every stroke precisely where he wishes it to land and to cover the whole bottom with well spaced stripes. He has an uncannily accurate eye." His Lordship glanced up to see Greenwood waiting patiently with the cane still poised over Brenda's bottom. "Ah yes. Sorry to interrupt Greenwood. Do carry on."

"Yes My Lord." Greenwood adjust his stance slightly and then brought the cane down for the second stroke. Brenda convulsed heavily against the straps and cried out in pain. She was obviously the vocal sort Lord Castlebridge thought to himself. A lot of the girls in the Hall tried, in common with his wife, to bite back their cries during the first strokes. Naturally it never lasted long before the mounting pain finally broke their resolve and they gave vent to loud shrieks. Some however yelled their heads off almost from the first stroke. It seemed Brenda Brideshead belonged to this latter category.

His Lordship's observation was confirmed over the next few strokes for Brenda's cries grew ever more shrill and desperate with every line of scorching pain to crease her tormented rear. By the seventh or eighth stroke she was screaming to the full capacity of her lungs and her caning had barely begun! Roger glanced in fascination at the imposing figure of Greenwood as he caned his wife. His demeanour showed not the slightest hint of pleasure or sadism but simply a detached, dispassionate attention to duty. You felt he would have shown the same face whilst serving cocktails at one of the Hall's receptions or examining the silverware on the dinner table. He seemed oblivious to the shrieking agony he was inflicting upon Brenda's convulsing body. It was all in a day's work to him!

Lord Castlebridge seemed a little dissatisfied with proceedings. "Perhaps a touch harder if you please Greenwood."

"Very well My Lord." The cane's swing became a whirling blur and Brenda's screams took on an even more demented quality.

Nobody was bothering to keep a tally of the number of strokes applied. Greenwood's numerical accuracy was phenomenal and, if charged with delivering a hundred strokes, then one hundred would be exactly the amount that his victim received. The cadence of his rhythm was uncanny too; almost metronomic, with machine like precision and every stroke as hard as its predecessors. Roger tried to keep a mental tally of the strokes in his head but he kept losing count as he watched his wife scream and writhe under the measured beat of Greenwood's cane.

Part of him felt perhaps he should be feeling sorry for her but there was something deeply exciting about witnessing her punishment; a dark pleasure in watching her pain he had never known in himself before. She was jerking violently every time the cane impacted on her rear and struggling futilely against her bonds: her face red and contorted in pain as she threw her head from side to side under the cane's assault and filled the library with her howling wails. Already her body was showing the toll of her struggles against the straps holding her to the caning stool for it was shining with sweat from the exertion.

Lord Castlebridge was keeping up a commentary on Brenda's punishment by way of educating his junior business partner. "You'll note Roger that Greenwood is spacing the strokes out evenly across the target to make sure that every part is properly covered." Roger could see the point. There was a distinct line of unmarked flesh between the angry red weals of the cane he could see but, even as he watched, Greenwood landed the cane solidly into the unmarked region to raise another fiery welt with unerring accuracy. Roger wondered feverishly just how many young ladies had had to suffer under the ministrations of the butler's cane for him to have achieved such masterful proficiency.

"You'll also observe Roger," His Lordship continued, "That Greenwood doesn't just confine the strokes to the buttocks. It is a rule of thumb in this house that the backs of the thighs are caned equally with the bottom. The region on the back of the thighs is particularly sensitive and any strokes applied there are extremely painful." Roger could believe it. His wife's screams rose to a particularly ear piercing note whenever the cane cut into the soft flesh of the back of her legs. The backs of her legs were already well marked with ugly raised weals. As he watched Greenwood delivered a scything stroke precisely into the crease separating Brenda's buttocks from the top of her thighs. Roger winced at the frantic howl drawn from his wife at the searing agony of that frightful delivery into such an acutely sensitive zone.

Brenda had never known pain like it in her life. Straining with all the strength of her body at her bonds, her earlier humiliation in her nakedness before witnesses had long since ceased to be relevant. Now her entire world had narrowed down to the cadence of the cane upon her flesh and the waves of unbearable agony it left in its wake. The torment just seemed to go on and on; a relentless, merciless infliction driving her over thresholds of endurance, and beyond the bounds of reason, towards madness. The leather straps were chafing at her skin as she struggled wildly in their embrace against the agony in her bottom and thighs. Her throat felt sore from her rasping screams and she was nearing the point of exhaustion. She couldn't seem to see clearly any more for her eyes were swollen with tears and her tangled hair was clinging to the sides of her wet face. The suddenly it stopped.

Lord Castlebridge looked at Greenwood in surprise. "What's the matter Greenwood? Why have you stopped?"

Greenwood was looking at the cane in his hand critically. "I'm afraid My Lord that this cane appears to have broken. I shall need to replace it before continuing."

"Oh I see. It seemed sound enough before."

"Yes My Lord but occasionally one does find a cane with some hidden flaw in the grain which can be quite difficult to discern under a superficial examination and only reveals itself when being used in severe punishments."

"Well are there plenty more in the cabinet Greenwood?"

"Oh yes My Lord. There are several similar suitable instruments. I shall replace it immediately."

"Well carry on then Greenwood."

"Yes My Lord."

As Greenwood walked over to the cabinet to choose a new cane Lord Castlebridge took the opportunity to walk over to Brenda to examine her and reassure himself that she would be able to take the full complement of cane strokes allotted to her. She was lying limply over the caning stool; with her chest heaving. At least she seemed to be taking advantage of the temporary respite to gasp air into her lungs. His Lordship placed a hand beneath her chin and lifted her face to examine her. Brenda had certainly been seen to better effect than her current appearance. Her face was red, swollen and streaked black with the ruins of her eye-liner and mascara down her cheeks. He moved the tangled mass of her hair away to peer into her eyes. They were wild, full of pain and swollen with tears but at least he could detect no sign of imminent unconsciousness that would have caused him to order the beating ceased. “Well young lady,” he growled at her, “I hope you’re learning your lesson.”

Brenda sobbed and looked at him pleadingly. “P...please My Lord.... no more... I... I can’t take it!”

Lord Castlebridge grunted. “I’ll take that as a yes then shall I.”

Greenwood cleared his throat. He was back in place behind Brenda holding a new cane. “I have replaced the implement My Lord if you will permit me.”

“Excellent. How many more has she to come Greenwood?”

“The lady has received a total of fifty seven strokes My Lord. She has a further forty three to endure to fulfil the full sentence awarded her My Lord.”

Lord Castlebridge nodded grimly and stepped back. “Very well then Greenwood. Pray continue!”

“Thank you My Lord.” Greenwood raised his arm and brought the new cane down viciously across Brenda’s tortured rear and the caning recommenced.

The latter part of Brenda’s caning was the worst of all. She had exhausted herself in her earlier struggles in the straps and now she just lay placidly over the stool, twitching feebly each time the cane found its mark. Even her loud screams had lost their earlier frantic quality to be replaced by an almost continuous keening wail and pathetic sobbing. There were tiny pools on the parquet beneath her face where her tears had dampened the polished floor and there was a drop of mucous on the end of her nose. Inevitably, by this stage, Greenwood had run out of clear spots to land the cane and many strokes were landing on top of the welts already raised by earlier impacts. In places the surface of the skin had broken under these accumulated blows and tiny drops of scarlet were beginning to appear.

Brenda had descended into some terrible netherworld. All sounds in the room seemed to come from far away now; even her own cries of anguish seemed distant and remote as if being uttered by someone else. A red mist seemed to have fallen over her vision and the only thing registering in her consciousness was the constant throbbing agony from her rear quarters which felt, in her fevered imagination, to have taken on gargantuan proportions like some great swollen, inflamed scarlet contusion dwarfing the rest of her body. And still the cane came down to further exacerbate that dreadful pulsing pain from that swollen monstrosity.

The onlookers witnessed this final act of the drama in solemn silence; even His Lordship felt twinges of pity for the young woman in the closing stages of her ordeal. Roger was standing hypnotised, wanting on the one hand to rush to his wife to comfort her and on the other determined to see the frightful punishment to the bitter end. Lady

Castlebridge and her two maids could barely bear to watch.

Then suddenly it was over. Greenwood straightened up. “The full sentence has been administered My Lord.” he announced gravely.

Lord Castlebridge nodded in acknowledgement. “Thank you Greenwood.” He murmured softly. He looked at Brenda carefully. She lay like a rag doll over the stool sobbing quietly now in the last throes of misery, still convulsing occasionally as if the cane was still striking her bottom. His Lordship had come very close to ordering the caning stopped during the last few strokes, sensing that the young woman was on the verge of passing out. But somehow she had endured; she had endured in agony and misery but endured she had. He felt a new respect for Roger’s wife. Apart from the one occasion during the interval when Greenwood had been obliged to change canes, she had not pleaded for mercy. She had taken her punishment. She had taken it with demented screams and floods of tears, but, nevertheless, she had taken it without pitiable pleas. That in itself was admirable. Roger had reason to be proud of his wife. She had demonstrated an inner core of fortitude hitherto unseen beneath her outward appearance of frivolous triviality. Allow that inner strength to come to the fore and flourish and much could be done with this young lady His Lordship thought. It was often the case, he considered, that a person’s true character could be revealed through the test of ordeal and hardship.

Thoughtfully he took Roger’s arm and led him

around to examine the beaten wasteland of Brenda's rear. "Well Roger," he noted, indicating the swollen mass of scarlet weals that had once been the pristine, unsullied surface of Brenda's pert attractive bottom, "that is what a well thrashed backside should look like!"

Roger stared in horrified fascination. From the middle of her thighs to the top of her buttocks, the cane had left barely an inch unmarked by the livid welts of its ministrations. It seemed incredible to Roger that his wife had managed to suffer that without falling into a dead faint. She normally made a drama if she merely pricked a finger or broke a nail. Yet she had taken this frightful beating. And Roger was certain of one thing. She had taken this beating to save his job and possibly even their marriage; sacrificed herself to agony for the sake of a greater good. From deep within him he began to feel a slow swelling of pride in the woman he had chosen for his wife.

Almost as if reading his thoughts, Lord Castlebridge squeezed his arm. "I think your wife will be a much changed woman for this Roger. Once she's recovered from her punishment I suspect you'll scarcely recognise her as the foolish girl she was before. I think you can be well pleased with her. She conducted herself bravely and took her punishment like a lady. You ought to be proud of her."

"Yes sir," Roger mumbled.

Lord Castlebridge peered at Brenda's bottom. "A little blood there but nothing too bad Roger. She'll heal well enough though she won't be sitting comfortably for a day or two that's for sure." He turned to his butler. "Excellent Greenwood! Capital job!"

"Thank you My Lord."

His Lordship nodded at Suzette and Maria. "Well you two girls had better release Mrs Brideshead now. She can have half an hour kneeling against the wall to recover then you can take her away to bathe her and see to her contusions."

The two pale faced girls curtsied. "Yes My Lord."

"Good and treat her gently do you hear. Greenwood! Is there any more cognac in that decanter? Mr Brideshead and I could use a fortifying drink after all that."

"I shall attend to it immediately My Lord."

"Good, good! Come Roger let's take a seat while the girls see to your wife. Don't worry about driving home by the way. I'll get one of my drivers to take you and your wife home in one our cars. I'll get one of them to drive your car home tomorrow."

Lady Castlebridge felt a great swelling of love for her two girls as they ministered to the pathetic beaten figure of Roger's wife. They were two little angels of mercy, soothing and comforting her as they gently released her from the caning stool and supporting her as she tried to stand unsteadily on treacherously unstable limbs. With the kindest of consideration, they helped her to the bench along the opposite wall where the household tradition determined that she spend half an hour kneeling on the bench with her face to the wall and her hands on her head as a final token of her disgrace. Brenda took the required position submissively, weeping softly to herself with her rear now a single throbbing ache, turning purple with bruising.

Lord Castlebridge was in a conversational mood now that the formalities of Brenda's punishment had been attended to. He was showing Roger the cane that Greenwood had used on his wife. "Greenwood makes these himself Roger." he was telling him. "Swears by these leather handles on them. Says they afford a much better grip when using them. He can't be doing with those old fashioned curved handle canes you used to see in old schoolrooms. Says the only reason for the curved handle is to allow them to be hung up and they're useless in fact to allow a decent grip on the thing. Instead he attaches a leather loop to the handle to hang them by. It's important to hang your canes up and in a dry cabinet. They tend to warp otherwise."

Roger nodded, reflecting that this was one of the most bizarre conversations he had ever had; quite in fitting with the entire evening in fact. "I see sir."

"Yes I'll see that you have a couple of samples to take home with you Roger and perhaps a couple of good leather straps as well. You should have the necessary tools about the house to maintain discipline Roger. Tell me, is that big loft in your house still unused?"

"Yes sir. I've just been using it to store a few things in."

"Excellent. I know this chap down in the village; carpenter he is... excellent craftsman. He built a replica of the caning stool for a friend of mine. Perhaps he could pop over to your place and build one to install in your loft. That'll help you keep your wife on the straight and narrow!"

"Thank you sir. I shall certainly consider it."

"Do so Roger. I've demonstrated the standards of discipline I expect from you and I'll expect you maintain them. With a caning stool as a deterrent in your loft your wife will think more than twice about repeating her recent misconduct I assure you."

The conversation continued in the same vain until Lord Castlebridge glanced at the clock against the library wall to note that Brenda had served the obligatory half hour in shame on the bench. He nodded to Suzette and Maria. "Girls would you bring Mrs Brideshead over here a moment?"

Brenda seemed to be recovering slightly. Her bottom was still an aching misery but at least she managed to walk unaided across the library albeit very stiffly. She stood naked before His Lordship and her husband in silent despondency, her humiliation complete. Lord Castlebridge looked at her not unkindly. "Well Brenda you've been punished so we'll say no more about the matter. I hope this has been a lesson to you." Unable to speak Brenda merely nodded miserably. "Good girl" Lord Castlebridge told her before turning to the two maids. "Girls, would you take Mrs Brideshead along to the bathroom, bathe her and tidy her up? You'd better put some ointment on her bottom as well while you're about it. No need to take her clothes. Her Ladyship will put them in a bag for her." Lord Castlebridge hesitated for a moment. "Oh one other thing before you take her girls. Roger I noticed that your wife is... well a little... how can I put it...a little hirsute around her privates. Do you approve of this?"

Roger was taken by surprise. "I... I hadn't really thought about it sir. I suppose she is a little bushy but aren't all ladies a bit hairy there?"

Lord Castlebridge shook his head. "Not in this house Roger. I don't approve of excessive topiary at the garden gate I'm afraid." He gestured to his wife and the two girls, "Come here you three and lift your dresses." The three women complied blushing with embarrassment. "Now drop your knickers girls and show Roger here the approved pubic adornment in this house. Meekly the three women obeyed and displayed themselves to Roger.

Roger was astonished. All three had perfectly smooth crutches completely shaven of any hair. He found the sight stimulating in the extreme. "I see sir." he mumbled, leaning forward for a better look. "It's er... most appealing sir."

"Exactly Roger. Far more attractive don't you think and cleaner too!"

"Yes sir. Quite sir."

"Well, with your permission Roger, I'll get the girls to shave your wife while they're bathing her. I think you'll find it much more aesthetic."

"I'm sure I will sir."

"Good that's settled then. Run along girls and attend to Mrs Brideshead here. Cynthia, would you collect Brenda's clothes please? I have a few items I want to pick out for Roger from the punishment cabinet."

As the two girls led Brenda away Roger looked puzzled about something. "Er why did you want

Her Ladyship to put my wife's clothes in a bag sir?"

"Ah I was coming to that Roger. Now that she's been punished I want to underline her servility and submission to your will Roger. To that end I want you to take her home naked. It's getting dark now and you'll be quite private in the back of one of the limousines. In fact Roger I want you to keep her indoors for the rest of the weekend and under no circumstance allow her to get dressed until Monday. Will you do that please?"

"Of course sir but I'm not quite sure what your intentions are. Is it merely extra punishment?"

"Partly that Roger but also partly to emphasise the new relationship that I think you'll find emerging between you. I've had the chance to observe your wife closely Roger and also your demeanour toward her. I think you've been letting her down Roger."

"In what way sir?"

"Your wife is a naturally submissive young lady Roger. She craves a strong hand; firm guidance to place certainty and security into her life. You've been failing her there Roger. Give her a dominant hand to lead her and she can begin to shine as truly a wife you can be proud of. Fail to provide her with that and she'll merely drift away at random seeking dominance among other men as she has so clearly been doing. Now that you've been seen to have her punished Roger the whole dynamic of your relationship has changed. Once she recovers from her beating and, assuming you exert your dominance over her, then you'll scarcely recognise the loving and attentive wife she'll become in place of the social gadfly she was before. She *wants* you to dominate her Roger. She craves that and without it she'll be deeply unhappy and be unable to find fulfilment in her life. Not every woman is the same Roger nor every man designed to dominate a woman. Quite the reverse in fact; but a submissive person needs that submission to somebody they love and respect to find contentment and safety in their life. Your wife is just such a woman Roger. The question is whether or not you are just such a man to provide her with that. So keeping her naked and inside for the weekend has more to do with you than it has with her; it's a way to train you to provide your wife with the domination she desires and, if I may be so bold as to suggest, the love she deserves. Do you understand what I'm trying to say Roger?"

Roger nodded "I think so sir."

"There are people who desire to surrender themselves in slavery to somebody above all else Roger. They are easy to train for they are already willing to learn that role. Far harder is to train a wise master or mistress to own them. That's the difficult bit Roger. You have a lot to learn."

"I see sir. I shall try my best."

"Good chap! Now come over here for there are some things I want to show you."

The brandy decanter had taken considerably more punishment by the time that the two girls led Brenda back into the library. Her appearance was much improved. The girls had bathed her, washed and brushed out her hair and repaired the damage to her face, applying cosmetics skilfully to restore her lovely features back to some semblance of their glory. Roger's attention however was drawn to her groin for she was now cleanly shaven, the skin baby like in softness above her sex. Her bottom was still of course ugly with swelling and bruising, and would be for some days to come, but nevertheless she looked more beautiful than Roger had ever seen her; a beauty somehow enhanced by the meek solemnity of her face and posture. He had never seen her more desirable.

Lord Castlebridge glanced at the clock. "Well it's getting late Roger. I'd best get Greenwood to rustle up a car for you. Before that however we'll attend to those matters we've been talking about. Come here please Brenda." Obediently Brenda came to stand in front of His Lordship. "Turn around and put your hands behind you back please." he commanded. She took up the required position and Lord Castlebridge took a pair of leather cuffs and bound them to her wrists before fastening them together by means of a clip behind her back. He turned her around gently. "You're being sent home naked and bound as a further penance Brenda." He told her and another thing. Kneel down please and open your mouth."

Roger was astonished by the way his wife meekly obeyed the instructions without question or argument and further amazed as she raised no protest as His Lordship took the ball gag, pushed it between her teeth and fastened it in place with the buckle on the strap behind her head. "This is to remind you that you landed yourself in trouble by opening your mouth Brenda." Lord Castlebridge told her. "Now one last thing." With that he produced a leather collar with a chain attached to it. He handed it to Roger. "This is properly your job Roger." he told him. Maria held up Brenda's hair as Roger fastened the collar about her neck. The atmosphere in the room seemed charged with significance as he completed the fastening as if some important milestone had been crossed.

Lord Castlebridge nodded in satisfaction. "There now. She's ready to take home Roger. Greenwood, would you go see to Mr and Mrs Brideshead's transport please?"

"At once My Lord."

Brenda knelt subserviently on the floor in front of them, her eyes lowered demurely and the chain hanging in a loop from the collar about her neck to her husband's hand. Beside Roger on the table was the bag containing her clothes and the canes and straps His Lordship had gifted to him. Brenda looked so beautiful in her penitent kneeling position that Roger felt such a burst of love and desire for her he thought his heart would burst.

Presently Greenwood returned to announce that their car was waiting. Roger stood and Brenda rose awkwardly to her feet on the end of her chain to accompany him. Lord Castlebridge had a final word for her however. He stood to take something from the punishment cabinet and to show it to Brenda. Her eyes opened in fear. It was a long single tailed whip fully seven feet long. "Now I'm hoping you've learned your lesson Brenda." he told her, "and that we shall see no repetition of your recent behaviour. If however your husband decides that your behaviour is still unsatisfactory and has occasion to return you here for punishment you may expect to feel this! Do you understand?"

Unable to articulate through the gag Brenda could only nod. His Lordship grunted in satisfaction. "Excellent. Well Roger it has been perhaps a difficult evening with some unpleasant duties to perform but I hope we can all start afresh from here. Now mind what I said about the regime for this weekend and I shall expect a full report on Monday."

"Very good sir."

Lord Castlebridge shook Roger's hand "Well you'd better be off now then." he told him. His Lordship watched Roger lead his wife out on the end of her chain with enormous satisfaction before turning to his wife. "I'm going down to my study for a couple of hours Cynthia." he told her doubtless you'll want to turn in."

"Yes Rupert I rather think I will."

"Good well don't wait up for me old girl. I have things to do and I'll be at least a couple of hours so I shall sleep in my own chambers."

Alone again in his study Lord Castlebridge leaned back in his armchair and placed his feet on his desk in great pleasure. He had liberated the cognac decanter from Greenwood and determined to drain it over a fine Havana cigar. He had been less that truthful with his wife. There was nothing demanding his attention in his study other than a couple of hours of privacy for himself. Doubtless his wife would take his absence as an opportunity to play with her two girls. She must think him simple if she thought him unaware of her leisure activities with those two little darlings, he thought to himself with a chuckle. He didn't begrudge his wife her little playthings however and he was always very careful not to catch her red handed with them until such time as it pleased him to do so.

For his part Lord Castlebridge stretched at ease in his chair and swirled the cognac around in his glass, savouring the aroma of the fine brandy with his nose. All was well in His Lordship's little empire. He listened in pleasure to the sound of an owl hooting in the poplars lining the drive and leaned back in contentment. Order was restored and all was right with the world beneath the hallowed eaves of Castlebridge Hall.

THE END

Lightning Source UK Ltd.
Milton Keynes UK
UKHW041153090920
369614UK00003B/120

9 781786 953704